Unreal

strange & quirky tales

MARION WRITERS INC.

ISBN: 9780646948133

Cover artwork, cover & interior design: *LRB Publishing Services*

Acknowledgements

Marion Writers Inc gratefully acknowledges the assistance of the City of Marion Community Grants Program for this publication. Many thanks to Marion Cultural Centre Library and Signatures Cafe for providing meeting venues.

Lisa sat quietly, sensing this was not the time to tell her parents.
Her father was right—Gavin was changing. He avoided light in
the daytime, he disliked breezes, he slept a lot of the time,
seldom washed and was more interested in the things in his
jars.
Absent Without Permission Marilyn Linn

Bleak winter days of dullness. A crow's presence on a limb.
Embodiment of sadness, as the weather closes in.
The Crow Anne Foggo

Being a time traveller's assistant wasn't what Wesley had
anticipated, but it made sense that even supernatural powers
needed organisation. He wondered if Veronica ever tired of
time travel. Being a Superhero wasn't all it was cracked up to be
as far as he could see.
Travails of a Time Traveller's Assistant Linda Brooks

An ancient naked man sat on his rock listening, not to the
chirping of birds or the rustle of the trees. He listened deep
within... He created a sacred place where he could feel the spirit.
The tribes-people visited and talked respectfully. He had them
dance and sing in that sacred place hoping someone else might
also be able to feel what he felt.
Backyard Spirit Michael Dwyer

I have a longing, one that has been with me since that day in
the market in Denpasar so long ago. It's an ache in my chest. It
feels as though someone reached in, grabbed my heart and
ripped it out.
The Longing Travis James

A wall of water surrounded her and in it she saw the faces of her ancestors, as if they had been taken from the family photo album.
The Ancestors Jen Mackenzie

The magistrate struck his gavel on the sounding block and waited for the babble in the packed courtroom to subside. 'Dominic De Gaulle. You are accused of causing grievous bodily harm to Humpty Dumpty by pushing him off a wall during the Grand Parade. How do you plead?'
The Chicken and the Egg Alex Yates

'Bunyips don't scare me,' I said, walking into the shallows to prove it, knowing *you* would warn me if there were any about. Becky's dad had strung the cages to the back of the dinghy. We all helped drag them onto the sand. They were chock-a-block with yabbies, clinging onto each other and clacking loudly.
In My Mind Beverley Rainsford

He heard the floorboards creak in the passageway. There it was again. A dragging sound followed by a distinct thump, approaching slowly, stopping at the bedroom door. The door squeaked open.
Karma Haydn Radford

Ariadne heard a familiar tune on a piano—Rachmaninoff's second piano concerto. The music came from across the road. Her ginger cat, darted past. Ariadne looked up at the open first floor window. The cat disappear inside. Determined to find out more, she pulled the heavy iron handle of the gate when a voice from behind startled her.
Ariadne's Story Athena Zaknic

Introduction

A few years ago I had the privilege of being asked by the Marion Cultural Centre Library to start a writers' group. I wonder if the people who turned up that first day had any idea of the tradition they were about to start. Of course, members come and go in any group, but a trusty few stay, encourage others to join, and create and maintain ideals and camaraderie, before they know it, they are the proud owners of a second anthology—each member playing their own part in their own special way.

Unreal - strange & quirky tales from Marion Writers Inc is a worthy production of dedication, enthusiasm and downright hard work. Ten different authors ply their craft, both individually and together, each unique in voice and style. There are writers that are emerging in confidence and form and are not afraid to experiment! It's an amazing journey through futuristic societies, literary mash-ups, perfect poetry and plain old fashioned spooky tales! Linda Brooks, Marilyn Linn and Travis James mix strong stories with bold, no-nonsense prose.

There are no better masters of spooky stories than Alex Yates, Haydn Radford and Jennifer Mackenzie. Beverley Rainsford is not shy of a clever twist in a tale that will draw you in and leave you gasping. Last, but not least, Michael Dwyer and Anne Foggo bring a gentleness of approach to balance energetic Athena Zaknic's high speed ride.

This is a book to be picked up again and again, each time to discover a powerful phrase, tempting twist or prosaic passage. You will be kept guessing, chuckling and ultimately satisfied.

Marion Writers are to be congratulated on their vision and form. Each and every one of them is a proud tradition-holder of this marvellous enterprise.

Long may they write!

Sue Fleming
Creative Director & Writer
January 2016

Welcome:

Welcome to the anomalous and peculiar world of Marion Writers.

Have you ever:

—wondered how time travellers manage without their assistants.

—wondered how anyone could be so careless as to lose his shadow.

—wanted to follow a cat to a concert in a thunderstorm.

—wondered if Gran really did have second sight.

—pondered if there's a secret ingredient in coffee.

—wondered whether messing with the truth messes with your Karma

—wondered how many aliens are living among us?

—wished you had your own fairy at the bottom of the garden.

—thought aliens might have coloured spaceships.

—wondered if you'd been given a particularly bossy guardian angel.

—wanted to be transformed into an eagle but...

—wondered if books talk to each other on the shelves when no one is there.

—been lost between the covers of a book, and found a different world between its pages.

Many people are sure their internal view of the world is sane and logical. The rest of us are not so sure. We, Marion Writers, have allowed our imaginations to roam.

Meeting monthly we critique one another's stories sympathetically because our stories hold a little of each author's soul. And through the years our writing has flourished as the imagination is released and ideas are shared.

As you are about to discover these quirky sci-fi, horror, fantasy and adventure stories embrace black and light humour, strong characters, clever twists and more.

Michael Dwyer 2015
President
Marion Writers Inc

Index of authors and stories

Linda Brooks

Linda caught the eye of a publisher when her humorous short stories found critical acclaim on the ABC website, The Making of Modern Australia. She has written *A curious & inelegant childhood*, several fiction novels, and written and illustrated children's books, been published in anthologies: *Coastlines* (Southern Cross University), *Wood, Bricks & Stone* (Catchfire Press) and *Grieve* (Hunter Writer's Centre).

Reality suspended

The books had sat side by side for so long that no one noticed what had happened, least of all the housekeeper, Mrs Campberwell, whose duty it was to clean and maintain her master's library. That dreary obligation had been neglected of late, due to Lord Dainsbury's propensity to confine himself to the warmer rooms in the North Wing.

This circumstance led to Mrs Campberwell taking the liberty of ignoring the library altogether, which was just as well because that august woman would never have taken the strain of realising that two of his Lordship's First Edition hardcover classics had, in fact, become one volume.

Mrs Scarlett Butler, however, was made of sterner stuff. Throwing off her initial shock and confusion at her mysterious conveyance to another place, her resourcefulness came to the fore. She perceived the superiority of her new surroundings to her beloved estate of Tara, in every regard other than pure sentiment. Upon finding herself in a new establishment, she decided to make the best of things. Settling in an elegant crimson chaise longue with her green ball gown draped to show her figure to its best advantage she looked around the room. The books trembled.

In a far corner of the room, Mr. Fitzwilliam Darcy was engaging in a tense conversation with Miss Elizabeth Bennet. Scarlett coughed loudly. The pair ignored her presence. There was something almost lover-like about their exchange and yet they appeared to be at odds.

When Miss Bennet stepped back angrily Scarlett rose quietly and crossed the room. This Mr Darcy was a handsome devil. Fluttering her fan, she flirted with him outrageously. Even though Mr Darcy appeared to be a man of few words, things were progressing beautifully until the arrival of Rhett Butler. Scarlett was elated, but rather than pay attention to his wilful wife Rhett became entranced by the wit and charm of Miss Bennet. Scarlett stamped her foot. She would not be bested by a country miss, English rose or no. The books shook. When Heathcliff slipped into the picture with his brooding intensity and careless ways Scarlett was diverted. Here was a man to match her. She had just caught his attention when the voice of a child intruded. It was a Miss Mary Lennox seeking Misselthwaite Manor. Her arrival was closely followed by Huckleberry Finn and the slave Jim who was instantly mistaken for Othello.

A dense noise erupted. The authors of those famous works arrived and began to argue loudly. The library shelves began to shake as the books battled to combine. The ruckus attracted Mrs Campberwell, who fell in a dead faint upon opening the library door.

Travails of a time traveller's assistant

Wesley stood outside the office of Goodwin Investigations & Recovery Agency. It was an old stone building in an upmarket area of the city. He was early for an interview as personal assistant. The Goodwin Agency was prestigious. The hours were flexible and the pay rate was more than generous. He loved being an artist, but even though his paintings sold well, the money was irregular.

Taking a moment to check his appearance in the large glass windows, he realised he should've had a haircut. He put a hand up to tidy his hair and saw a daub of paint on his hand. So much for a good first impression.

While the Estefans' Café & Restaurant opposite was enjoying brisk trade, there was no-one on the Agency side of the street. Wesley wondered how many other applicants would be attending. Squaring his shoulders, he pushed open the ancient timber and glass door. A bell tinkled in the back room. He looked around. The office resembled something out of the Forties with its antique furniture.

A tall elegant woman was shuffling papers on a mahogany desk that dominated the room. 'Drat,' she said, as a sheaf of papers hit the ground and slid across the floor.

Wesley stooped to retrieve them.

'Don't worry, young man. I'll do it later. I need to pick them up in a particular order.' The woman tucked a stray strand of coal black hair into an off-kilter bun that was held in place with a pencil. 'I'm Veronica Goodwin, owner, investigator, dogsbody, you name it. And you are Wesley Brent.' She twisted around, eyes scanning the room. 'Now where are those ... darn, can't find a thing. Nice to meet you.' With a wide smile she reached out and shook his hand. 'Well, Wesley Brent, you can see my drastic need for a personal assistant. She gestured at the shambles of paperwork on her desk. 'Please take a seat.'

Wesley folded his lanky frame onto the chair. He opened his mouth to begin the spiel he'd been rehearsing for days, but Veronica had flipped open the laptop computer and was tapping random keys.

'Wretched thing. I hope you understand it,' she said. The computer beeped into life. Veronica squeaked in surprise. She shuffled the papers on her desk. 'Oh there they are,' she said, placing a dark rimmed pair of glasses on her face with a satisfied sigh. 'I hope you'll like it here, Wesley. The job is yours.'

'Oh? I thought this was an interview. The employment agency told me to bring these.' Wesley held up a black folder.

'Daft lot, those agency people. I have all your information on file.'

Wesley's eyebrows flew up. 'You do?'

'Naturally. Um, cyberspace, internet, you know.' She pointed at the computer, eyeing it suspiciously.

'Ah, the agency sent my information. I see.'

Veronica frowned, then seemed relieved. 'Ah yes, that must be it.' The computer pinged. Veronica shut the lid down. 'I see you're quite the artist.'

'How did you know that?' Wesley squirmed in the chair.

'I've seen you painting the mural for the Estefans' café opposite.'

'Oh, of course.'

Veronica leaned back. 'I believe you are perfect for the job Wesley. You have a good reputation for confidentiality.'

'But I haven't worked as a personal assistant before.'

'You're much too humble Wesley Brent. Always have been. Why that fiasco back at University, with the student newspaper— you only wanted to protect Sara, of course, sorting the petty cash theft by replacing the money yourself. Wouldn't have worked the second time though.'

'Say again.' Wesley sat bolt upright. 'How can you possibly know any of this? *Were you there?* This is bizarre.' Wesley mopped his forehead with a handkerchief that had seen better days.

'Oh Wesley, the world is never quite what it seems.' Veronica smiled. 'I'll start from the beginning...'

Wesley slumped in the chair.

Veronica brought him a glass of water. 'I'm a time traveller Wesley, you know—travelling to different...'

Wesley choked on the sip of water. When the coughing fit ceased, he viewed the woman opposite him with watery eyes and a shocked expression.

'Oh dear. You look like you want to run out the door. Please stay and hear me out, Wesley.'

'Don't think I could stand if I tried.'

'I'll give you time to take it all in. I can almost see the cogs in your head turning. You were like that back then too.'

'So you *were* there. I don't remember seeing you. Were you invisible?'

Veronica laughed. 'One Superpower at a time please!'

'Wait a minute—you said something about the *second* time. There wasn't a second theft.'

'Ah Wesley, but there so very nearly was.'

Wesley leaned forward, alert. 'Ah. I know. A week after the money went missing I was working late on the artwork for the paper. There was an almighty noise, but there was nothing out of place. I would've searched longer but Sara phoned me from the hospital. Her father had broken his leg.'

Regret flashed across Veronica's face. 'Were you alone in the building, Wesley?'

'Well yes. Everyone had gone home. Wait on, there was just a janitor, some new woman. Said she hadn't seen anything, kept her head down. Funny sort of a ... Oh my god, *that was you!*'

Veronica nodded. 'There was a reason you were protecting Sara. Apart from the massive crush you had on her. You thought she knew something.'

Wesley flushed.

'Oh, you poor dear. You're still carrying a flame for the girl. After ten years. It was a noble thing to do—replacing the money.

Ill advised, but noble.'

'Sara was the only other one with the keys to the office. But I knew it wasn't her.'

'And you were right. She didn't. It was her father.'

Wesley's face turned white. 'Her father? *Bill took it!*'

The phone jangled. Veronica picked it up, and in perfect diction spoke into the mouthpiece. 'You have reached the office of Goodwin Investigations & Recovery Agency. This is an automated message. We apologise for not being available, but your call is important to us. Please leave a message and we will return your call.'

Wesley's mouth dropped open. 'You're good, you think quickly. Guess you've been doing that for centuries.' He held up a hand. 'Don't tell me. I don't want to know. But, how did Bill take the money?'

'Simple really. Crime often is. He only had to stay hidden in the staff toilets in the main administration block at closing time, then slip out the fire exit afterwards. Security wasn't great in those days, as you'll remember. He was disappointed to find less than $50 the first time so he decided to make another attempt.'

'Oh dear, this is starting to make sense. Bill was always short of cash. He would borrow from Sara. I'm pretty sure he had a gambling problem. But I never thought he'd do something like that. Sara can't possibly know. It would break her heart.' Wesley ran tense fingers through his hair. 'I was just returning from the toilets when I heard the ruckus. What on earth did you do to stop him?'

'Simple. I came rattling past with the cleaning trolley. Bill got a shock, lost his balance, then ran off.'

'But his broken leg?' Wesley rested his elbows on the desk, watching Veronica intently.

'Bill's, er, shall we say *loan officer*, was waiting for the money in the car park with a couple of thugs.'

'Bill said he'd stopped to help a homeless man and been attacked. My God, the lies he told.'

'Bill was trouble. I think that's why Sara has that bad boy attraction thing going on. It's often the way, it's why nice guys like you finish last.'

'Just for once I'd like to finish first, with Sara. Do you think...'

A loud knock at the door deferred any words of wisdom Veronica may have offered. It was Estella Estefan with two pizza boxes. The aroma filled the room. Wesley's stomach growled.

'Estella, how kind,' said Wesley, ushering the woman inside with a grin, 'but where is Veronica's pizza? She'll be hungry too.'

Estella slapped his arm. 'You tease an old woman too much, Wesley. One is for your new boss. You have the job? Yes?'

Veronica nodded and laughed.

'Good,' said Estella. 'Don't you be letting this one have your pizza, Senora. Like a horse he eats and yet he stays thin and handsome. It's enough to make a woman cry.'

After they had eaten, Veronica became crisp and businesslike, filling Wesley in on his duties. She swept around the room, clouding the air with exotic perfume as she detailed his role and explained the filing system and client records.

Wesley's eyes widened when Veronica told him that her previous assistant, Evan, was still back in time. 'He's lost, somewhere,' she said, quickly wiping a tear aside. 'So you see, you really must be very particular.'

Veronica handed Wesley a handwritten list.

Stay close.
Follow instructions immediately without question.
Don't act on any other matter except the case in hand.
Don't interact with anyone you know unless it's unavoidable.
If you speak to anyone, say nothing to affect their destiny.

Worry lines creased Wesley's forehead as he contemplated the last line. He held it up. 'I hope you don't expect me to eat this Veronica, because I don't think I could fit it in after all that pizza.'

'You've been watching too many movies.' Veronica laughed. 'And they said you were boring.'

'Who said that?' Wesley shrugged. 'Never mind, I don't want to know.'

'Precisely why I hired you, Wesley Brent. Tomorrow we begin...'

As soon as Wesley walked through the door the next morning he saw Veronica buzzing around the room. She retrieved a small card from the file with a photograph attached.

'This one will do today, Wesley.' She tapped the client card with a red nailed finger. 'Are you ready?'

The first mission wasn't what he had anticipated. He'd expected to be involved in preventing some terrible event in history—a bombing or a plane crash at the very least. But that first assignment had been a tense waiting game in a seedy downtown bar, late on a wintry night a mere ten years in the past.

A middle aged socialite had paid an exorbitant fee for Veronica to intercept her husband, an ageing Don Juan, from meeting his current mistress. Because the wife had no way of knowing the exact moment her husband had met the dazzling creature who'd become his latest lover, Veronica and Wesley endured a long wait.

The prospective mistress was in an upstairs room singing a collection of sultry ballads. The cheating husband didn't arrive for hours. Finally, he swept through the door bringing an icy blast.

Veronica flicked a cigarette lighter near the fire sensor. A narrow flame rose and flickered unnoticed. The alarm shrieked. Chaos reigned. Patrons screamed and shoved, desperate to escape. Wesley seized the man's arm and ushered him into a waiting taxi. The would-be lover was on his way in a matter of minutes, none the wiser.

Over the next few months Veronica relaxed. Wesley was sure she had grown to trust him. She didn't comment any further about Evan. Perhaps he had failed to stay near her when they were on a mission or broken one of the other rules.

They slipped into an easy routine. Veronica gave him a brief outline of the mission ahead along with concise instructions. Then they entered the creaky lift at the rear of the building; their conduit to another time. Veronica used an ornate fob watch to select the parameters of their destination. When they stepped out of the lift they were at the precise location and time she'd programmed.

It was Wesley's job to arrange incidentals. Detours and meals were often necessary and it was also his role to source the correct money and maps. Wesley hadn't imagined these necessities, but it made sense that even supernatural powers needed organisation. Once they were on assignment, Veronica had bigger things to worry about.

When the mission was complete, Veronica signalled to Wesley. Taking the small black mobile he'd been given, he pressed *. That summoned the lumbering George with their taxi. The taxi was different according to the era, but it was always George who collected them. When they were in the taxi Veronica tapped the watch. They were instantly back in the office lift.

To Wesley's disappointment, the assignments continued to be mundane. They stopped Mrs Damson's Labrador wandering from home. They travelled back to the day Mrs Wiltshire decided to dye her hair a fiery red. One assignment had involved showing up at a ritzy hotel to remind a young bride-to-be to pick up her handbag containing a ridiculously expensive engagement ring. They sent Mrs Beverley home early from the supermarket the day the decorators were due, forestalling a 'truly hideous colour choice' by her husband who was taking revenge on his wife for inviting her mother to stay.

Wesley consoled himself with the thought that his new life was the closest he'd ever come to being a hero. Anyway, he had plenty to keep him busy. There was research in the library building to ascertain whether the client was attempting to use their services for criminal purposes. 'Better safe than sorry,' Veronica said. And there was always the weather to check.

Winter slipped into spring. Wesley finished painting the mural for the Estefan's and had arranged to meet Sara at the café after work. The mural was a vibrant portrayal of life in Italy. Wesley had painted all the Estefan family members from their village, sitting at tables and dancing in the square.

The last rays of the sun slanted onto the rooftops. Wesley whistled as he walked. He was looking forward to spending the evening with Sara. The café was their favourite eatery. It was full of the aromas of Italy and throbbed with the hum of friendship and life. Inside, the stucco walls were painted a muted crimson. The floor was covered with black and white harlequin tiles that shone and sparkled all day. Estella achieved this by rolling out the ancient metal bucket and mop at least half a dozen times a day.

Wesley greeted them and sat with Dimitri.

'Oi, that woman, she makes me tired,' Dimitri said. 'She will wash away the tiles and we will have just concrete left.'

Estella swished the mop in the direction of her husband. 'Why are you sitting old man?' she asked. The men exchanged sly looks and grinned. 'Oh, you have finish our mural Wesley? May I see? Dimitri does not let me have even one peek.'

'Come woman, and stop your bellyaching at me.' Dimitri led the way outside.

Estella wiped her apron across watery eyes. 'Bellissimo Wesley! Where did you learn such things? It is just like home.'

Her voice was rich and caressing. She embraced Wesley. 'Why did you not wait for Sara? Oh see, here she is now.'

Wesley turned. Sara had left her corporate image behind. Her long chestnut hair was loose and she wore a casual sundress. She looked like sunshine, young and free. The image of her in the twilight reminded him of the first time he'd seen her at their University orientation event. He found it hard to breathe and hoped she didn't notice.

Estella bounded to meet Sara and swept her aside. 'Ciao bella. Is not the mural Wesley painted bellisimo? He is wonderful. And so are you, coming to help an old man with his accounts. Grazie, molte grazie.'

Estella cleared the tables while Wesley swept the floor.

Dimitri sat at the corner table with Sara. He leant over the old ledger stained with sauces from the kitchen. The old man watched the earnest young woman tally the accounts; her eyes alight with enthusiasm.

'How can you love numbers on a page?' Dimitri said, 'when there is so much more.' He placed his hand on his heart.

Sara looked up. 'Are you all right, Dimitri?'

'Of course, cara. It is *your* heart I think about. It is for you time to fall in love.'

Sara laughed. 'I have had too much love, Dimitri.'

'You have had too much something, I think. But it is not too much love.'

'I keep getting love wrong, Dimitri.'

'It's not the love you get wrong cara, I think you maybe get the wrong man.' Dimitri removed his glasses and wiped them on his red handkerchief. 'Don't listen to me. I'm just an old man who wishes everyone happy.' He glanced across at Wesley who was emptying bins while Estella sang to the pigeons crooning on the beams under the awnings. 'Come, enough work. Wesley, join us and celebrate.'

Dimitri brought two bottles of red wine, dragging Estella from her cleaning on the way.

As the chill of the evening fell, Estella lit the candles and coaxed Dimitri to dance with her.

Wesley took Sara's hands and led her to a space between the tables. He pulled her close. 'This will have to be a very slow dance Sara, there is not much room.'

'The mural is wonderful, Wesley,' said Sara. 'I don't know how you've had time for it. You've been helping me set up my new office on top of your own work. It's a big step for me, starting an accountancy practice on my own. I couldn't have done it without you, you know. You're my best friend.' She gave a nervous laugh. 'I don't know how you've put up with me. All those tears I've cried on your shoulder over some stupid man.'

Wesley struggled to find words, but couldn't. Instead, he kissed the top of her head. Just one tear for me, Sara. I'd give anything for you to cry one tear for me, he thought.

Sara put down her glass and took Wesley's hand. 'I have something I want to ask you.'

Wesley's eyes searched hers.

'I would really like you to be my partner in the business. We're a great team.'

Disappointment formed a lump in Wesley's throat. 'I'm

sorry, Sara. I have a job,' he said, his voice thin. 'It's, well it's important. I help Veronica find things and people, make a difference.' He spun her around, forcing a smile and cursing his cowardice for not revealing the real reason—that it would be unbearable to see her all the time, loving her as he did. Friendship would have to do.

'I'm sorry. I shouldn't have asked,' she said.

He blanched at the pain in her eyes. He smiled to soften the words. They continued to dance, but the mood between them had changed. Estella chided the grandchildren for peeking when they should have been in bed. Wesley heard the deep rumble of Dimitri's words of love to his wife and her laughing response. He experienced a sharp pang of longing and drew Sara closer.

The next morning Wesley woke early and ran a hasty hand through his hair. His mind was annoyingly foggy. He must have had too much red wine. It had been a magical evening. While Sara was in his arms he had almost hoped ... but now he had to focus on the day and the next mission. When he arrived at the office Veronica briefed him. Derby Day, Kentucky, 1974. A father had gambled away his daughter's college fund on a 20-1 horse named Patience.

At the races they recognised their target from the photo his daughter had provided. The man was waiting for the betting booth to open. He paced, patting a fat wallet. Veronica tipped a glass of wine on him and began a long-winded argument with him. He missed the queue.

'That's great,' said Wesley. 'All over quickly.'

'I wish it was that simple. There are three more days of the racing carnival.'

'Oh. He's still going to blow his money, isn't he?'

Veronica sighed. 'If he gets the chance. We'll have to stay. Tramping around a soggy racetrack isn't my idea of fun but we have to see this through.'

Wesley wondered if Veronica ever tired of time travel. Being a Superhero wasn't all it was cracked up to be as far as he could see. He booked them into a small Bed & Breakfast near the racecourse.

Their man was a vain and superficial creature who seemed to care only for fancy clothes, inane conversation and copious quantities of whisky, and survived on a few hours' sleep at night. Wesley could quietly murder him. God only knows what *that* would do to the cosmos. Veronica was in fine form. She managed to prevent the man from placing a single bet. After the final race was run, the two time travellers sat exhausted in the refreshments marquee.

'The last three days have been the most terminally boring of my entire life,' said Wesley, resting his head on the back of the chair.

Veronica dropped her wine glass.

Wesley put a hand on her arm. 'Veronica! You're as white as a ghost!'

Veronica's hands shook. Her eyes were fixed on some point in the straggling crowd that was streaming towards the exit gates. All at once she was off, throwing herself into the jubilant arms of a well-built man with a thatch of blonde hair. Spinning her around, the man rained kisses on her neck.

Wesley froze.

'What the...? Veronica! You'll mess with the time space continuum thingy.'

Veronica turned to face him, her arm firmly around the man beside her. 'It's all right, Wesley.'

'No it's not! This can't be good, it's dangerous. It's against the rules—*your* rules.' He reached for his notebook. It wasn't in his pocket. 'This can't be happening. We'll never get home.'

'Wesley, stop. This is ... my assistant, the one I lost, remember?'

Wesley gaped at them. 'Evan?'

'Yes, Evan. Evan *Goodwin*.' Veronica placed a gloved hand on Wesley's arm. 'Everything is as it should be, Wesley.' She peeled the glove from her hand, revealing a wedding ring. 'This is where I belong. Here with Evan; in the past.'

'Oh! I see,' he said, scratching his head. 'Actually, I don't see at all.'

Veronica smiled a soft smile of regret. 'Think about it, dear man.'

'Oh, my! So, I'm from the future.'

'Yes, Wesley dear.'

It was quiet in the taxi with George. Wesley watched the outside world blur by the darkened taxi window.

'What happens now, George?'

'Whatever you choose, Wesley.' George handed him the fob watch; the key to going home.

Wesley looked down at the watch. The legacy of time travel

was now his to accept or reject. He could be the next Superhero if he wished.

Wesley handed the watch back. 'You tap it George. I'm going home. For Good.'

He ran from the lift. The office didn't even warrant a sideways glance. He needed Sara, wanted her. He would accept the partnership. She might come to love him. It was worth the chance.

Sara stared out into the darkness. The city lights blinked mutely. Where on earth was Wesley? He'd been gone for days. She wound her hair around tense fingers, wavering between anxiety about his safety and anger that he hadn't called. Now and then, she wiped salty wetness from her face.

She thought of everything they'd been through together. All the times he had been her calm and stable rock. She thought of the weeks she had spent with him after his parents died, when he hadn't been able to face the world. She'd made him get up and keep going, forced him to eat, gone through every corner of the cottage he grew up in, sorting all the possessions of his parents' lives. She remembered all the times they'd helped each other shift. When had her feelings turned to love? How had she ever been content with friendship with this wonderful man? The one who never let her down. She wept bitter tears. Tears for Wesley.

Finally, as the pink dust of dawn intruded she curled into a ball on the sofa and fell asleep.

There was a loud rap on the door.

She flung it open.

'Sara, you really must remember to check who's at the door before you ... Oh no, you've been crying.'

She crushed him to her.

'Who hurt you this time?' Wesley murmured against her ear. 'I'll kill him.'

'Then you will have to kill yourself, you idiot! Where have you been? I've been worried out of my mind!' She rained salty kisses on him.

'I haven't been gone that long,' he said. 'What do you mean? I'm the one who hurt you?'

'Do I have to spell it out for you Wesley?' Sara's eyes sparkled.

'Yes, please.' Wesley drew her closer and manoeuvred them to the couch where he pulled her into his lap. 'Spelling would be great. I've always liked spelling. Did I tell you I won a spelling bee once...'

Sara silenced him with a lingering kiss.

'I think you misspelled that. You may have to do it again.'

Sara laughed. 'I love you.'

'It's about time. I've loved you for ages.' Wesley smiled. 'Now *do* stop interrupting a perfectly good spelling lesson.' He returned her kisses with all the passion of those hungry years.

Who's out there

Who's out there?
Who? I mean who?

Who wanders and prowls on dark starry nights
when nested birds have ceased their flight
vague sounds stir tense slumber
while I make lists for the plumber

Who scratches and taps with random beat
then taunts the night air before faint retreat
with frivolous regard for my weary plight
while I turn away from dawn's early light

Who flutters and flaps with keen disregard
is there a wild animal in my back yard?
seeking to hunt, or just to perturb
rushing and bashing my sleep to disturb

Two cats are a courtin', (or something quite like it)
if they keep it up, I'll tell 'em to hike it
a tom plays the sax, another strums guitar
come daybreak, they'll bolt with many a scar

The book guardian

Ephram Garibaldi pressed a rheumy finger on the panel at the back wall of the library. He watched the glass doors glide shut, while the security shutters rolled smoothly down, cutting out the twilight.

'Silent as the grave, young Mark,' he said.

'At least white noise has been eliminated in this new world.' Mark tapped his foot.

'You say that like it's a good thing.'

'Well, isn't it? I mean...'

'Ah, young Mark, if only you had seen the world I lived in. Leaves fluttering down, birdsong.'

'Ah music.' Mark reached for the electronic panel.

'No. Not that manufactured e-streaming stuff.' Ephram waved a dismissive arm. 'The real thing.'

'Sorry.' Mark let his arm drop.

'It's okay, Mark. I'm not upset with you. And I won't go on about how things once were. You've heard enough of my ranting about the things we lost in the Third Age of Technology.' Ephram sighed. 'It was bad enough losing the natural world, but now they are pressuring everyone to buy tickets to the

Palindrome in the Ancient Natural Order Museum to see a "3D experience of the past in living visual and sound"! Pfft, *living*, it's an insult! A theatrical production is a poor replacement for what we had before humanity destroyed nature.'

Mark rocked on his feet, his eyes alight. 'But we have the books, you saved them. Well, some of them anyway.'

'Shh, young Mark. We don't discuss this here remember.' Ephram put a hand on the boy's shoulder. 'What a wonderful thing it is that I found you. You're a wonderful help,' he said, eyeing the surveillance cameras. 'Well, it's time to leave.'

Mark smiled and winked. Ephram frowned. The boy really must learn to be more careful in the library. Every movement and sound was recorded. The consequences were unthinkable. All those years of reclaiming books would be undone. As it was, he'd only saved one copy of each book and sent the rest to the relevant Transformation Centres. He didn't dare take more. It was hard enough to hide them in the early days, and it was getting harder.

Ephram took the small disc that locked the room, tapping it as he ushered Mark out the side door of the library and headed to the lifts. Mark flicked furtive looks down the corridor and Ephram rolled his eyes. The boy was so obvious. He waited until the lift doors had closed before pressing B for the lower floor instead of M for the main entrance level. Their subterfuge must not be detected.

'I found a student trying to download more data than his quota today,' Mark said. 'Don't they realise every byte is detected the minute it's accessed? There are signs up everywhere. Then there was one girl who had two storage units on her arm and tried to get double by using different access points. She'd borrowed her boyfriend's Xephar, she thought he had reconfigured it to her ID code, but our systems are too good for that. There's a penalty, so I deactivated her Xephar for three months.'

'Was she the one with the bright pink Xephar?'

'Yeah, pretty cool.'

'I don't know why anyone wants coloured ones. I still haven't got used to those things. It's crazy to think they've invented a device that is magnetised to bone. They look like bandaids.'

'What are bandaids?' asked Mark.

'Well, they were ... Never mind, go on with your story.'

While paying scant attention to Mark's nervous chatter, Ephram allowed his thoughts to wander. How he'd scoffed when people predicted books would be obsolete one day. What a fool he'd been. He'd made an application to DAFTU the Data Antiquities & Securities Technology Union for the Canberra Library & Data Bureau to become the central site for sorting and processing books.

That had been Ephram's first win. All the books came to him for collation. He put the earliest edition aside. Then he selected a good edition of each book and carefully wrapped it for the courier to take it to the Commonwealth Ancient Arts Museum & Gallery. The rest went in the boxes and were labelled RECONCEIVING before being sent on. When he had tried to access the online data for the reconceiving process, he'd found nothing.

Not even the usual overblown government propaganda. Nothing. If only he knew what was happening to the books. What did reconceiving mean? He hated the word.

The lift door slid open. They entered the basement. It was a cold dark labyrinth with a dank odour. Mark was silent as they walked past the storage units for broken technology and outdated tablets. These units were only accessed twice a year when the equipment was sorted.

There were so many unused storage areas due to outsourcing of the cleaning and maintenance work that Ephram had had his pick of rooms thirty years ago. Not much had changed down here since then. No one came if they could avoid the place.

'We can't stay long tonight,' said Mark.

'I know,' said Ephram, 'there have been cuts to the number of Xubers. Where would we be without those driverless, soulless transport modules?' He pictured the sleek half-moon-shaped vehicles that glided around the city in their grooved tracks.

'Yes, they only come every hour now, but they do take you to your own door.' Mark shrugged. 'I've never known anything else. I guess it was different for you.'

'Yes. There was a strange satisfaction in having a steering wheel in your hands, deciding your own destination, even changing your mind if you felt like it. Stopping off at the grocery store.'

'Grocery store?'

'Before your time, boy. Food and nutrition lists weren't always collated from an electronic setting on the pantry and fridge, beeped in and out and then delivered.'

'Wow, I wondered where food came from. Cool.'

Ephram sighed. He pulled out an ancient key and opened a dark grey door. Most of the storage rooms had been updated to electronic entry, but there were a few that had been overlooked, and this room was the largest of those with keyed entry. Ephram had overheard one of the retrieval maintenance men ask 'What kind of technology opens those doors with the funny holes?' Ephram had smiled. The room would be left alone.

Mark set his Xephar alarm. They sat in silence with their chosen books from the shelves.

Ephram caressed the leather binding of 1984, a limited edition, much like the one he had hidden at home in the apartment he'd shared with Evelyn before she died, and now Bluebell. At least he still qualified to have a cat. What pets would replace cats in the evolution of technological living? Cockroaches? He chuckled.

'Can't get into it, Ephram?' said Mark, pointing at his companion's unopened book.

'No, must be showing my age.'

'It's great they let you work over 85 isn't it?'

'Used to think so, boy.'

The Xephar alarm sounded.

Carefully replacing the books the two men left.

It was chilly at the Xuber exchange. They greeted two men who were also waiting. One wore a suit and a pin on his lapel that showed he worked for the government. The other wore casual clothes and had a large box on a trolley.

'Bit small,' said the suited man, eyeing the box.

'They're flatpacked,' the other man responded. He turned to Ephram. 'When is the next Xuber to the city?' Ephram looked at his Xephar, but Mark was quicker and already had the correct screen up.

'You might have trouble putting that thing in the Xuber,' said Mark. 'What is it anyway?'

'Mark!' Ephram frowned. 'Sorry, the impudence of the young.'

'It doesn't matter,' said the man. He looked at the suited man for approval. The suit shrugged. 'We're launching these on the international news tonight. I'm the artist who's designed them. It's so exciting. We've been working on these for years, using all the recycled books.'

'The books?' Ephram paled.

'Yes. I have a prototype sculpture in here. There were so many proposal ideas, but this was Senator Citrine's brainchild.' The artist gestured towards the suited man who smiled in the deferential manner of the supremely vain. 'I just executed the idea. I had to conduct a lot of research. These are magnificent, if I do say myself. Senator Citrine has been assisting with the funding. Actually, it's all down to him really. Right from the concept that paper books were an unacceptable drain on the environment.'

'Really,' said Ephram, turning to the politician. 'Senator Citrine. The man of the hour. Humph.'

Ephram looked at the box. 'Where will these, um, sculptures be displayed?'

'Well, naturally they will only be placed in areas of top

security,' said the Senator.

'Like Parliament House?' Ephram glared.

'Well, yes and a few select residences.'

'Yes.' The artist leaned forward. 'It's exciting. Naturally the Senator has one. Along with his environmental award.'

The senator looked at his shoes.

'Amazing,' said Ephram. He stood in front of the senator. 'May I ask what the books have been reconceived as?'

'Ubertrees.' The man smiled widely.

'Uber *what?*' Ephram's voice was a tense squeak.

'Trees.'

Ephram snapped. His fist connected with the Senator's jaw.

'Not bad for eighty eight,' he said as Mark dragged him away.

Michael Dwyer

Michael is most interested in the future of this planet, its people and the life supporting natural environment. He is fascinated by the myths and beliefs by which we live, the fantasy world and the economic-growth-forever policy among other things.

He loves to cycle and has ridden across the Nullarbor. He finds fast weekly rides both healthy and social. He is a regular at the community garden and loves to read and write. This story is the prelude to a full length book of a backyard spirit, world events and an ex-drug addict finding his way in a small town.

Backyard Spirit

An ancient naked man sat on his comfortable rock listening, not to the chirping of birds or the rustle of the trees. He listened deep within. There was a feeling and he thought of the feeling as a separate spirit and he believed this spirit was aware of him.

The ancient man created a sacred place where he could feel the spirit most strongly. The tribes-people would visit and talk to him respectfully, sometimes receiving medicines from the plants he grew nearby. He had them dance and sing in that sacred place hoping someone else might also be able to feel what he felt.

But time passed and those people in their very old land died and new people came from across the sea and settled there, in and around the ancient man's sacred place. The spirit bided its time waiting for someone else who would again have the feeling.

Maisie was young, healthy and looking forward to a long life with lots of bustling children when she and Cecil settled into Burravale after World War II. They were eager to get on and were just able to raise the money to buy the house with a government war loan. Their three-bedroom house had a large backyard which seemed to them, to be in a particularly fertile, healthy spot.

'We've been married for a year now,' Maisie said one Sunday morning after a passionate night, 'and I'm still not pregnant. Why Cecil? It's not as if we don't try.'

'Yes, we do try,' said Cecil smiling and stretching luxuriantly. 'It's a bit odd isn't it, but let's wait a little longer before we start to worry.'

'And then we will go and see Doctor McPherson, not that I think he knows much,' said Maisie cuddling up close.

On returning from church and changing out of her Sunday best, Maisie strolled into the garden to do a little weeding. The early spring vegetables were coming on well. She felt at ease in the garden as she thought about the baby she would have one day and how it would play in the garden; it might eat a snail or two. She smiled.

'Hello,' came a voice from behind her.

'Heavens child, you startled me,' said Maisie turning to see a toddler standing behind her.

'I play in your garden?' asked the tot of perhaps two or three years.

'You live across the road?' asked Maisie. 'Of course you can play here. But it is the same as your garden.'

'Your garden is more funny.' The toddler hurried down the garden path as fast as his legs would carry him, laughing and waving his arms about. *Why is my garden more funny?*

On Tuesday morning, Maisie went next door where the many wives and mothers were meeting for a cup of tea. It was anything but quiet with crying babies, laughing toddlers and screaming, racing children. Maisie nursed the babies and helped out where she could. She listened, hiding her irritation with a smile when mothers advised the best and easiest way to get pregnant.

Two children broke in on Maisie and a group of mothers, 'Mum, can we go to Auntie Maisie's garden?'

Maisie was now an unofficial auntie.

'No. Play here in this garden,' said the mother.

'But it's better at Auntie Maisie's garden. It's so funny. We want to go to her garden.'

'Tomorrow. Now, outside you go.'

'I think we better meet at your place next time, Maisie,' someone said. 'Seems the kids like it better there, I've no idea why.'

The morning cup of tea gathering moved to Maisie's place more often than not. Maisie felt the children were a lot quieter and less trouble there. She would sometimes walk outside and see the children shrieking with laughter in a circle in the same spot in the middle of the garden. Once or twice, Cecil popped home from work and he too was delighted to see the children running about the garden.

'Soon Maisie soon, we will have our own little ones.'

Maisie and Cecil were regulars at the Returned Soldiers League club of a Saturday night where they would meet with some of Cecil's friends.

'Don't look now,' said Denis, Cecil's close friend sitting at one end of the table, 'There's Baxter and he's rolling drunk already. Someone needs to make that man straighten up and step into line.'

Cecil slowly stood up from the table, 'Excuse me everyone, I'll take Baxter outside for a walk.'

He left the crowded table and walked over to the drunk and increasingly obnoxious, Baxter. Cecil took his arm and steered him outside into the cool of the evening. Cecil turned to face Baxter and stared into his face.

'What are you doing Baxter, annoying people and getting into arguments? Shape up and be a man. Look at yourself, no job, sleeping on the footpath, getting locked up for the night .... You're drinking far too much and you can't hold down a job. What's wrong with you? You were alright during the Africa campaign in Tobruk.'

'I know, Cecil. I don't sleep too good. It's the memories. The war won't leave me head.'

'We all handle it and you can too. You just have to get a grip on yourself and straighten up. There's nothing more to it than that. Are you seeing a doctor?'

'I don't need no doctor, I got plenty of medicine, right here,' Baxter smiled as he produced from his pocket a half sherry bottle wrapped in a paper bag.

'That won't help at all. You go and see a doctor! You hear me? And Baxter,' Cecil paused, 'are you staying away from kids? You know what I mean; I was there in Syria you know, and I got you out of that brothel.'

'I don't do that anymore, honest, Cecil. That was the war.'

'It better be,' Cecil paused for a moment. 'You remember when you and I were in the sand storm and they came and killed lots of our mates? I kept you alive when I bayoneted two of them in the bloody foxhole. You know what I can do, don't you Baxter?'

'Uh, yeah, Cecil ....'

'Get a job, stop drinking and keep away from kids. Make no mistake Baxter. You were in my unit and we all looked after one another. We still do. You are still in my unit. Don't ever forget that. Now go home. And Baxter, see a doctor.'

Cecil watched as Baxter stumbled off down the dim street. He turned and re-entered the club, wondering if he had done any good. He walked into the hall and the music, noise and cigarette smoke floated around him, soothing him a little. 'Denis, I badly need a drink, pour me a beer would you,' he said as he reached their table.

Denis turned to his wife, Irene then to Maisie, 'Drinks anyone?' He counted raised hands and disappeared making his way past the tables and people towards the bar.

'How is he?' Maisie asked Cecil when he was seated beside her.

'Pretty bad.'

'What did you talk about, what's upsetting him?'

'We talked about how he's getting on. And we harked back to our memories of the war, when we were in action together in the Africa campaign.'

'Did he listen?'

'I think so. I certainly think I gave him something to think about.'

'That's very sweet of you dear,' she said as she laid her hand on his shoulder smiling. 'I'd like to go home soon. So you can plant something before we go to sleep.'

'Shh. Someone will hear.'

Maisie was on the committee of the Country Women's Association. The CWA was a major social focus of the town and the farming community's women; they would meet and discuss events away from the beer and male mentality.

'Dorothy is back, she came in last night on the train,' said Joan, during a committee meeting. 'She might be prepared to come along and tell us of her adventures.'

'Where's she been?' asked Maisie, the relative newcomer to the group.

'She was a nurse in the war, she spent some time in New Guinea then returned home only to take passage to India. And now she's back but I don't think she's settled down yet,' someone else said.

'She lives with her brother. I could drive out to Cooee Springs and ask her if she will speak,' said Joan.

There was general agreement from the committee and so, two weeks later there were more than the usual numbers at the CWA monthly meeting waiting to hear Dorothy's story of travel and adventure. Dorothy was tall and confident looking, dressed in a light coloured skirt and top but wearing a brightly coloured shawl, clearly a souvenir from her travels.

Maisie sat in the front row and listened as Dorothy spoke of her visit to an 'Ashram' in India to learn from a 'Sri Bhagavan'. She was mystified as Dorothy explained how we are all part of the same one being, much the same as a bee is part of a hive, '...which is the creature, the individual bee or the individual hive?' Dorothy asked rhetorically. 'If one listens closely,' she said, 'one can feel the oneness of us all.'

These ideas perplexed Maisie but she liked the idea of the unity of everyone.

'Meditation is a method of getting in touch with the oneness of us. We learn to breathe in a way which opens our heart to the spiritual world,' Dorothy said to the puzzled audience. 'It is in the spiritual part of us that our oneness becomes so clear.'

In the buzz of conversation during the tea and coffee break Maisie approached Dorothy. 'I really didn't understand what you had to say. Would you like to come to my place for tea and a chat? I would like to talk more.'

'I'd love to come. I will be in town on Friday after the weekly shopping. Let's make it then.'

On Friday, Dorothy and Maisie sat on the veranda with a cup of tea. Before the conversation had really started, two small children walked into the yard.

One of them said, 'We want to play with Fairy.'

'Yes, away you go, talk to the fairy.'

Turning to Dorothy, Maisie said, 'The Smith children come here often to play with the fairy. They are sure there is a fairy in this garden.'

Maisie paused, then continued wistfully, 'I would love to have a little girl or boy to talk to the fairy.'

'That would be lovely, wouldn't it. There is time for you yet,' replied Dorothy looking at her, 'Perhaps the time isn't right or you are destined to do other things.

'Would you like to try a meditation exercise, Maisie? This garden feels to me like an exceptionally good place to meditate.'

Dorothy demonstrated a breathing rhythm to calm the mind. 'Concentrate on the breathing itself and let all other thoughts drift away.' She started a low chant and Maisie listened with fascination.

For the next ten minutes they were still and silent with only the coo of doves and the laughter of the children on the edge of their awareness.

'There really is something here,' said Dorothy breaking the silence. 'I feel it and the children do too. It's as strong as the experience I once had in India. Do you feel something?'

'There is contentment. But that's just from the happy children and the good weather, isn't it?'

'Perhaps. But I feel something different, special ...' She paused. 'I feel nothing like it out on my brother's farm.'

At that moment the two children broke into peals of laughter. They turned to look at the two women sitting under the veranda and one of the children screamed, 'Mr Cecil and Auntie Maisie, play here.'

'For a baby,' the other child said, slapping the ground she was sitting on. They burst into laughter again and rocked over backwards still laughing.

'They want you to play with Cecil right where they're sitting Maisie. I think they mean you're to make love to Cecil right there. And you will have a child, that's what the children and the fairy think.' Dorothy smiled. 'And so do I; this place is very special.'

'What? Is that why they are laughing? I receive lots of advice on how to get pregnant but that really takes the cake. Advice from a fairy. Oh dear, Cecil would be so embarrassed.'

'Perhaps they know more than we do. Maybe they are listening to something we can't hear.'

On a warm Saturday afternoon Cecil was working in the garden with his pipe in his mouth and a beer by his side.

'Now,' thought Maisie looking out the kitchen window. The aroma of the roast lamb from the oven said it was almost cooked so she turned the oven to low. She stepped quickly to the bedroom, stripped off her clothes and covered her naked body with one of Dorothy's silk shawls held by a string of flowers about her waist. The shape of her breasts and hips and her darker hair were barely hidden in the moving silk colours. She turned on the 'wireless' radio as she passed through the kitchen and sensually strolled outside. The gossamer shawl drifted about her naked body as she danced to the music. She surprised Cecil who, on seeing her, smiled broadly and put his pipe down.

'Hello Fairy. Let me give you a big hug. What mischief can we get up to now?'

Maisie guided Cecil towards the middle of the garden where the children always gathered. She encouraged his hands to wonder over her body and felt his heat and desire rise. It felt so good to be there with this man she loved.

'Give me a baby, Cecil.'

But then the world intruded. There was a sharp crack like a rifle shot as a car backfired. Cecil dived flat on the ground and put his hands over his head. His body shook and trembled with anger, 'No, no. Not again. The bastards! Get down, look out.'

She knelt down beside him, her shawl and flowers forgotten. 'It's only a car. Nothing to worry about Cecil, the war is over now.'

Cecil slowly sat on the ground, his chaotic emotions slowly draining away. 'Shell shock, they call it; bloody bad memories, I call it. The guns, the bombs, the stink and the blood. The churning. The Oh, so useless, damn stupidity and waste.'

The mood was lost and Maisie led him inside. She changed her clothes and prepared to serve the roast.

'Let's try again Cecil,' Maisie said days later, putting her hand on his arm. 'There is magic in the garden and Dorothy and the children say, if we make love in the garden, we will have a baby.'

'Hah, childish women's nonsense. We've been trying for ten years now and nothing. We're childless and childless we are going to be. You are what, thirty-three and almost past child bearing age? We've got to get used to it, that's the way it is and that's the way it's going to be.'

Tears rose in Maisie's eyes.

'Maisie, there are always lots of kids around the house,' he said softly reaching out to her hand over the kitchen table, 'Not ours but still ... I think we have to enjoy what we have.'

Cecil left for work and Maisie, again in tears, walked out to the garden. The day had become overcast with dreary clouds in keeping with her emotions. *What to do, what to do...*

Cecil and his friend Denis took to the road cycling and racing their bikes about the countryside. Denis had not gone to the war; he was needed on the land. Though their backgrounds were different they respected one another and enjoyed conversations about how the town should be developed and both liked to talk about the marvellous modern inventions like television sets and mains electricity. Their wives enjoyed one another's company as well; Maisie and Denis's wife Irene would often meet when the two men went off riding. Neither couple had children. Maisie thought their mutual childlessness drew them together.

One morning at the end of their ride and before they parted company, Cecil said, 'Let's have a BBQ this afternoon, Denis. I need a good long drink after the chase up the hill. And this baby issue is getting to me.'

'Good idea. I'll let Irene know. I think we are free.'

Cecil rode home and parked his bike in the shed then strode inside to give Maisie a sweaty hug. Maisie drew back with thoughts of the garden and baby making.

'Shall we have a barbecue this afternoon with Denis and Irene?' asked Cecil. 'We haven't had them over for a while and there are some chops in the fridge.'

'Good idea. I will make a cake for later,' she said trying to put their recent disagreement behind her. Barbecues were the only time the men cooked and her spirits lifted as she looked forward to a relaxing afternoon.

Around midday, Maisie heard Denis and Irene arriving.

'I thought I had enough beer but I'm short,' said Cecil

looking in the fridge. 'I'll drive down to the pub. Won't be long.'

'What about us girls?' said Maisie. 'Irene, go with him and find some of the fruity sweet wine we like.'

Cecil and Irene drove off leaving Denis and Maisie in the backyard.

'Come, I'll show you my climbing beans; they are going very well this year,' Maisie said as she led Denis out to the garden. They walked into the bright sunshine then something made her stop in the middle of the garden where the children liked to play. She turned to look up at Denis and felt a heat grow within her.

Denis said, 'I feel something wonderful here, Maisie.' He smiled, 'It's a beautiful day in this garden of yours.'

Maisie's heart fluttered. She was sure she heard something within, 'The father, here is the father. Go on, take his very good seed.' *I'm not the sort of person who gives in to a whim. I don't cheat; I have standards...* she battled with herself and turned away from him. She accidently brushed against him to avoid the rosemary bush and smelt his masculinity and felt her body insisting 'Yes, yes.'

'Denis, this garden is more naughty than wise. I have a huge attraction to you right now. But it's not right.'

'Then perhaps we'd better go and check how erect and powerful the beans are thrusting up.' His eyes twinkled and he smiled but made no move. Maisie strode down the garden to get some distance between herself and Denis. She moved behind some sweetcorn so as to partly hide from Denis' eyes. Denis stood where he was, still smiling, clearly enjoying the moment.

On a branch of the peach tree against the old fence, a male

dove tried to impress the female with its bobbing head and fanning tail wings. Maisie slowly walked back to Denis and stopped in front of him and was about to put her hand on his chest.

At that moment, Cecil walked onto the veranda, his arms full of bottles. 'Are you going to stand there all day while I pour beers on my own?' Cecil said looking from one to the other and back again.

'There's something funny outside,' said Cecil some days later as he walked into the kitchen after smoking his pipe in the garden. 'I get the urge to eat some of those strange plants growing at the back fence every time I walk past the middle of the garden.'

Maisie replied, 'Really? It must be the Fairy. Ask the children who come here. They think there is a fairy. Imagine, our very own fairy. Wouldn't it be wonderful. Why don't you follow your urge and see what happens?'

'What and poison myself? There's all sorts of things, even deadly nightshade down there. Fairies are for kids, not adults.'

Cecil put his pipe on top of the fridge and sat down at the kitchen table. 'There is something wrong here and I don't like it. I will build a new compost heap in the middle of the garden to stop all this nonsense. That or maybe I'll spray some power kerosene or sump oil on it.'

'Don't expect me to sit by if you start spraying sump oil in my garden,' Maisie said, raising her voice and getting up from the table. 'You don't know all the answers Cecil so don't act like you do.' She strode over to the sink and rattled the dishes.

'All right, all right. No poisons. But I will put the compost heap right there in the middle.'

Maisie, with angry tears in her eyes, walked outside. *Compost! Smelly compost on the best spot.* But a wave of peace rose and submerged her anger. *Perhaps the garden likes compost, good healthy compost, nutrition and new life?*

Her thoughts turned back to her own dull, grey future. *Why worry about a garden if there are no children? No children of mine playing in the garden. Barren.*

Cecil wasted no time in starting the new compost heap on the spot where the children formed their circle. A familiar youngster from further up the road walked in while Cecil was working and said, 'Hello Mr Cecil,' and immediately started helping carry cuttings to the new compost heap. Maisie watched from the kitchen window. Was the garden happy with the way things were going? She carefully watched to see the youngster's reaction.

'Chooky poo,' said the child looking up at Cecil.

'What?' said Cecil.

'Chooky poo, too. Chicky poo.'

Soon there was a large and growing compost heap full of cuttings of all shapes and sizes and fowl manure in the centre of the garden. Maisie saw Cecil and the child standing back and smiling proudly at their work. Perhaps everything was alright after all.

Not long after the compost was started, Cecil was working in the garden alongside Maisie, trimming back the old tomato plants.

With a little care a few more tomatoes might grow before the start of the colder weather. Suddenly Cecil groaned and doubled over with his head in his hands.

'Oh, my head, Maisie. I've got the grandfather of all headaches. It hurts so bad.' He straightened up. 'It's this garden, there is something poisonous here, I'm sure there is.'

'You are just working too hard. We've been at it since this morning. Come and sit down. It's not the garden. More like it's some of those poisons you use on the vegetables. Come inside and I will make you a good cup of tea.'

A half hour later Cecil's headache was almost gone and they were sitting quietly. Maisie was knitting and he began to talk about the business. He had three trucks now and business was good.

'I don't know where to put the new truck I'm going to buy. Maybe we could cement the backyard and I could park all four there. It would save me a lot of time,' he said, carefully looking at Maisie.

'You want to do what?' she said pushing her knitting off her lap and dropping a stitch. 'How could you? No wonder you've got a headache, thinking like that. Maybe the fairy has read your mind and is punishing you.'

'Alright, alright. But I don't like the garden. Have you seen the advertisement for the new house across from Main Street? Treloars are selling and we could buy it. It's got a vacant block next door and I could use the space to park the trucks and build a work shed.'

Twice more Cecil developed a splitting headache while

working in the garden. He came inside to talk to Maisie after the second bout and slumped down into his armchair.

'That's it, we buy the new house and move away from this damn place. We aren't getting any younger you know. The new place will be easier for me to work from too.'

'If you must, but we keep this house. We can let it out,' said Maisie turning to stare out the kitchen window. 'But I do like it here. Let's buy a television set instead and we can sit and watch it like other people and you can relax more. They say man is going to walk on the moon and we can watch it on the television.'

Cecil's health continued to fail and trips to Doctor McPherson were becoming more common. Maisie and Cecil also made trips to the city to see the specialist who agreed his heart was weak and his blood pressure was too high. His prescription list grew. Doctor McPherson advised giving away the pipe and drinking a little less but Cecil continued to drink and smoke as he had always done.

His gardening became less and less. He told Maisie, '... because it seems to bring on those damn headaches.' He still rose early though and struggled to work by seven to keep up with his thriving business. He tried to hide his weariness from Maisie but it was becoming more and more obvious.

'Maisie,' he said one day when feeling particularly poorly. 'We had better move house while I am still in one piece.'

She replied, 'The Treloar place is not so bad, but it needs a bit of a tidy up. I like it more now than I used to. And you like the block of land beside it, so...,' she paused and took a breath. 'Yes,

I think it's time we should move.'

'It's the best thing for the two of us. I will stop by the Dream Tugger Real Estate people in the morning and get this moving.'

The following day after a small shower of rain, Maisie was picking some spinach at the far end of the garden when she sensed a movement behind her.

'Oh, Jenny, it's you.'

Fairy doesn't want you to go,' replied the three year old.

'Doesn't she?'

'Fairy wants a mummy and daddy to live here.'

'Does she?'

'And the baby. You will be its Granny and Fairy will be its Granny,' the child smiled.

Maisie laughed. 'You've got it all worked out, haven't you Jenny?'

Jenny was silent for a moment then and with a frown on her young face said, 'I like to talk to Fairy. Fairy is lonely, Granny.'

'Then I better have a mummy and daddy come and live here when we go.'

'Yes. Then there will be a baby. Like my Uncle and Auntie's baby.'

'Does the Fairy want me to garden here when the house is rented? Do you think the Fairy will be happy if I keep gardening?'

'Yes, Fairy wants two Grannies for baby.'

Maisie smiled at the beautiful simple logic.

Six weeks later Cecil and Maisie were walking through their new house. 'The old lounge will fit there, and the side table will fit along the wall,' said Cecil pointing into the living room through the half open sliding glass doors.

Maisie sniffed, frowned and walked into the living room. 'It's a new house; it should have nice new furniture.'

'New-fangled stuff, waste of money. Our old furniture is perfectly serviceable.'

'We are going to rent the old place, remember. It will be much more attractive if we leave some furniture in it. And we can buy one of those televisions everyone is getting and put it over there,' She pointed to a wall in the new lounge.

A week later, some of Cecil's friends spent the day helping to paint the interior of the new house. A thankyou BBQ and beer followed. Cecil was sitting back with a pleased expression on his face when Maisie arrived after her walk from the old house. She went inside the new house to inspect and was impressed with the contrasting light browns of the walls and the very light pink ceiling. *Most fashionable,* she thought as she came outside smiling.

'Good job boys. Looks like we can move in now, Cecil.'

The following day, Denis and Cecil loaded the truck with the selected furniture to make the short trip to the new residence. In the afternoon the new kitchen table, bed and lounge were delivered from Main Street. And they were in. They had moved house.

Maisie was trying to adjust as she put clothes into her wardrobe and the linen in the press. As she started to put the kitchen cutlery in place, her mind drifted to the old house and the garden.

'I'll leave this for you to finish,' she called to Cecil who was in the shed. She strode out the front gate. There was a basket to retrieve and the beetroot seedlings to keep an eye on.

At the old place she picked up the light chair she had tucked under a tree and walked out near the compost heap. A warm tenderness flowed over her, quieting her unrest. *It is good here.* She felt so very peaceful.

Cecil's health deteriorated slowly though his headaches stopped in the new house. He began selling off parts of the business and made an effort to continue riding his bicycle more often.

Maisie continued to do the gardening at the old house. One day she was planting some capsicum near the compost heap with Jenny providing a hindering hand at her side.

'Is the Fairy here today, Jenny?'

'Yes. Fairy is saying things.'

'Is she?'

'Yes. Mr Cecil is sick, isn't he, Auntie Maisie,' said Jenny.

'Yes, he is not well.'

'Fairy says he would not take his medicine from the garden. That's why he's sick,' the little girl said matter-of-factly.

Maisie was shocked. How on earth could this little girl think of such a thing?

'And that's why he's not a daddy, too.'

'Oh, My ...' was all Maisie could say as she stared at Jenny. *Can a fairy make a man fertile?*

'Fairy is talking about babies.'

'I wanted a baby too,' said Maisie.

'When the mummy and daddy live here, there will be a baby,' she said with a smile.

'Then I hope the house rents soon, Jenny.'

There were few new jobs to be had in Burravale and the old house remained empty. One day when Maisie was in the backyard, there was a knock at the door.

'Anyone home?'

'Come round the back,' called Maisie.

A solid looking young man with fashionably long hair and check shirt appeared at the side of the house. He smiled and introduced himself. 'They said this place is for rent. I need somewhere to live for a year or two while the chicken works is being built.'

At Maisie's invitation, he walked inside and then around the garden. It appeared he was taken with the old house and garden. He stood at the rear of the property and gazed about with a smile on his face.

Just then Jenny skipped up the path.

'Hello Granny.'

'Hi Jenny. That man might live here,' Maisie said to the back of Jenny, who was running down the garden path. Jenny reached the centre of the garden and did a circle and pirouette with her arms spread wide. She then ran back to Maisie.

'No.'

'No? No, what?'

'No. He won't play with Fairy.'

Maisie was surprised. Why would the pleasant young man be

unacceptable to Jenny?

'I think he wants to live here, Jenny.'

As she said the words a wave of negative sentiment descended over Maisie. *Now why am I against this lad? He looks perfectly charming.*

The man approached them, smiling, 'Can I get back to you, Mrs Sexton? The place looks perfect. I'd like my girlfriend to see it.'

What to do, what to do? As the man stood beside Maisie, a magpie swooped down from behind and attacked the man with a warning cry. He ducked his head and raised his hands for protection.

'Oh, I'm not welcome then,' he said.

Even the birds don't think he belongs here, thought Maisie.

'I'm not sure I want to rent just yet. If you give me your phone number, I can ring later,' she said.

Cecil left and Maisie pondered why she had chosen not to have him. *Am I getting old and silly? Why doesn't Jenny like the man? I liked him. Am I trying to hold onto the past?* Later that night, 'Cecil, someone was interested in renting the old place.'

'Oh, good. About time too.'

'He was only looking,' Maisie replied, frowning.

Nothing remains the same forever and four years later, Maisie's life changed yet again.

Cecile didn't come home from his regular ride at the normal time and Maisie was not concerned until the doorbell rang and she glimpsed the police car through the window. Her heart dropped.

'Hello Ken,' she said, greeted Senior Constable Ken Lawrie.

'Maisie, I've got bad news.'

Maisie sat with her hand covering her mouth and eyes wide when Ken told the story. Cecil and his bike were found in the ditch beside Flats Road about five kilometres from home. There was no apparent reason for the accident. The ambulance driver thought Cecil may have had a heart attack while still riding.

Friends came by to express their sympathy as soon as word of the accident spread. In the days that followed, Denis and Irene helped with the funeral arrangements. The funeral was large for the town. Everyone from the Returned Soldiers League, Cecil's business friends and Maisie's Country Women's Association friends crowded the small church.

The comings and goings after the funeral kept Maisie busy for a few weeks then life began to settle down. Denis and Irene called by but there were pauses in the conversation. It was uncomfortable for all three and they called by less often.

Maisie was not alone in the town but she felt lonely. She often walked to the old house to quietly sit and listen. Bitterness rose. No children and now her husband of many years had died and she was alone.

He's gone, dead and I will follow him. Sooner the better. What's the point of it all? I don't know. But there was still the warmth about the garden which held her. Some things are meant to be and I must move on. One day it will be my turn. But not just yet.

'Hello Granny,' said a voice from behind her.

'Oh, hello Jenny,' Maisie said.

Time had passed and Jenny was four years older now. Maisie had been invited to her seventh birthday - my, how they grow so fast, thought Maisie not for the first time.

'You are lonely.'

'Yes Jenny, it's true, I'm lonely.'

'And the Fairy is lonely too. She wants a baby. I don't know why I think this but you will be its Granny and so will the Fairy,' the smiling Jenny said. 'You must have grandchildren in this garden because Fairy wants this.'

'Yes, that would be lovely.' And very soon now Jenny, you will forget all about fairies and the games you used to play.

Three weeks later Maisie was working in the garden and Jenny was copying Maisie as she pulled out weeds. Sometimes Jenny pulled out the newly planted leek seedlings too but Maisie didn't mind.

'It might be time for biscuits and a glass of milk. How does that sound?'

Before Jenny could reply, there was a thump and clatter at the side gate and a dishevelled big man appeared from the side of the house. He was staggering and clearly weaving drunk and he leaned against the veranda post for support. *Oh no*, Maisie's heart dropped, *not Baxter*.

'I've come to rent Cecil's bloody house. I been tipped out of my room.' He stared drunkenly at Maisie, 'You're his missus aren't ya. Well, I want to rent the place.'

'Hello Baxter. The place is already promised.'

Baxter stared at Jenny and seemed to have forgotten Maisie. He lurched down the path towards Jenny.

'Baxter, stop,' Maisie said and she grabbed his arm. He swung back and gave Maisie a shove which sent her sprawling over the newly planted seedlings. Maisie could smell the booze as he staggered onwards to the middle of the garden, towards the thoroughly frightened Jenny.

'Come over here girly, I got somethin' for ya.' He grabbed her arm and started to pull at her clothes.

'Mummy,' screamed the frightened Jenny, 'Mummy! Granny! Help!' she screamed. 'Fairy, Fairy, help!'

'Quiet, ya little bitch,' he yelled. But then Baxter froze. He slowly straightened up, releasing Jenny and raising his hands to his head as if he had been stung. He groaned and bent over and slowly rolled to the ground still holding his head. He began to yell and scream.

'The sand's in me eyes. Help me! They're coming over the top Cecil. The pain. Cecil, they've stuck me. Ah No. Cecil, No!' Baxter yelled now lying in a foetal position. Jenny stood well back holding her hands together against her chest and looking from Baxter to Maisie and back again. She turned and ran to the veranda but then stopped.

'Hello Fairy,' she said and then grinned. 'Granny, Fairy is here. It's alright now.'

Maisie struggled to her feet and rushed to comfort Jenny. She hugged her close but Jenny was laughing. Maisie took her by the hand, rushed into the house and locked the door. She watched through the window holding Jenny's hand who was also trying to see out the window. Baxter lay moaning and rolling on the ground still holding his head. After a few minutes, he became quiet and still. Maisie gathered up Jenny and strode out of the front door still holding Jenny's hand who, surprisingly, seemed totally unaffected.

'We have forgotten the biscuits, Granny.'

'I am taking you home, young lass, away from that nasty man,' she said as she walked along the street.

'The Fairy is nice. She smacked the nasty man very, very hard.'

'Fairy is certainly nice, Jenny. And strong too,' replied Maisie. *And how strong is a fairy? Strong enough to turn a man into a pathetic mess on the ground? Turn the terror in a child's delicate mind to something to be laughed off?*

On reaching Jenny's house, Maisie called to Jenny's mother. Jenny ran off to tell her brother all about it.

'Such a sad, broken, nasty man. He should be put away for good,' said Jenny's mother. 'I'll call the police,'

'And they had better bring an ambulance too,' Maisie said.

They sat in the lounge waiting.

'Cecil felt some responsibility for Baxter ever since the war. Shame Cecil's not here now,' she sighed. 'I think Baxter's days are numbered. He might even be dead now.'

Cars presently drew up and after a few moments, Constable Lawrie knocked at the door.

'Come in Ken.'

'Hi Maisie, Mary. That's about it for Baxter, we think. The poor sod looks like he's breathed his last, not that anyone will grieve his going. We saw far too much of him.'

'Is he dead?' asked Maisie.

'The medic said he looks like he has had some sort of stroke. Probably won't make it to the hospital.'

'Oh, dear, such a terrible business,' said Jenny's mother. In an attempt to restore normality, she rose and suggested, 'Let's all have a cup of tea.'

The atmosphere calmed as tea was poured. Jenny walked into the kitchen and announced she was going back to talk to the Fairy but her mother said it was time for her bath.

Maisie rose to go. Ken said he would walk her back to the house, not that it was necessary, thought Maisie. At the old house, she looked down the garden path to the compost heap then stooped down to gather up a few of her garden tools.

She stopped motionless. Soft gentle laughter wafted through her mind. Fairies, there are fairies, there really are. They arc real, very real. She looked about the garden, at the verdant trees along the fence lines with blossom sprinkled throughout, the thriving vegetable beds laid out in their orderly way with the huge stands of green broken by a few small ornamental flowers. She saw the familiar small parrots busily gathering what they could and the mynah birds jumping about as they always did. In one tree a magpie kept a watchful eye on everyone. 'There is something here in my garden here. And it's real, very, very real. Thank you for your help today, Fairy.'

Fundamental things stay the same but Oh my, how the world changes, thought Maisie, the day after her eightieth birthday. Eighty years and where have they gone?

Many of her friends from earlier times had passed on, Irene among them, and lots more were missing from the Country Women's Association. There were so few of the old faces at yesterday's birthday party. The chit chat and the casual cup of tea when they used to call in ...

Maisie walked to her old garden knowing the exercise did her legs good. Young Doctor McPherson thoroughly approved; he seemed to know a lot more than old Doctor McPherson. Today she planted some zucchini seeds and remembered when the Second World War refugees first introduced these strange and exotic plants. *Where is Dorothy now? Has she passed on?* She had kept in contact with Dorothy over the years though she was usually in faraway places.

Because of her influence Maisie continued to meditate and she usually practiced while sitting in a chair in the garden. Or was it nodding off, she sometimes wondered? No matter.

Such thoughts she had while meditating. The Fairy spoke to her and often laughed. Maisie thought it was laughing at her and the foibles of people. She asked the Fairy when to plant and she was sure she did better listening to this inner advice.

There were less young people about the town than there used to be, or perhaps she didn't mix with them the way she did when she was more active. She remembered the dear little girl, Jenny, who lived up the street so many years ago. Her family had moved to the city and she had heard nothing since. Then Hazel mentioned Jenny was returning to Burravale. She will be about thirty now.

One day there was a knock on her door and there stood a well-built attractive lass in jeans and shirt. It took a moment for Maisie to recognise the skinny little Jenny from all those years ago.

'You're back, Jenny! How good to see you. Come in, do come in.' They hugged and walked into Maisie's lounge.

'My, how you've grown. And seen all the world and what it has to offer too, I imagine,' Maisie was smiling broadly, holding Jenny's hands. 'Now you're here again. So lovely to see you.'

'Yes, back again. I think I will settle here in Burravale.'

'Oh, good. Are you married? Children?'

'No, none of that for me. Perhaps I'm too choosy,' Jenny said.

'Let's have a cup of tea; we can sit in the lounge. I have some cake; come and help me cut it up. You always liked my fruit cake.'

They made afternoon tea and sat in the lounge of Maisie's "new" house. The paint was old and faded now and the lounge was showing its age with small marks and patches picked up over the years.

'What have you been up to, Jenny?'

'Quite a bit, I went to Uni, graduating with an arts degree and then I worked for a big corporation. Lately I've been living up the coast with lots of other young people on a country property. The world is changing Maisie and it's all very exciting. Some call me a green environmentalist but I'm not sure what I am.'

'The world is certainly changing far too fast for me. Did you come across any fairies when living up north?' Maisie watched Jenny's face carefully. *What memories has she kept?*

'Oh, I remember we played with fairies when I was a kid at your old house. The Fairy used to laugh and have all us kids laughing too. Yes, I remember. Haven't spoken with any since, though I have mixed with people who talk like they see fairies all the time. Politicians believe in magic fairies.'

'Do they really?'

'Yes, they call them economists,' replied Jenny and they both laughed, though Maisie was puzzled.

'Shall we walk over to the old place?' asked Maisie.

'Yes, I'd love to. Then I want to go to the Chemist, I am hoping for a job there. Can you put in a good word for me the next time you're passing?'

'Certainly I will. Let me clear these dishes away and we will go. I must keep my joints moving.'

Jenny walked slowly with Maisie along the familiar streets. Most of the buildings looked the same, but more worn than twenty-five years ago. A few gutters were missing here and there. There were a few new houses with modern fake stone square fronts which seemed out of place to Jenny. They crossed the main street, past the Chemist on the corner and continued up the opposite side street. There was Maisie's old house, unchanged but needing paint and a few nails to secure some galvanised iron sheets on the roof.

'Has it been vacant all these years?' she asked.

'Yes, most of the time. I like to garden here so I didn't try too hard to rent it out.'

'I wish I had known. I have entered into a long lease for another place further up the street,' said Jenny.

'Oh, such a pity. But come round the back. I want to see if the garden still likes you,' Maisie said.

They walked to the backyard. Jenny saw the trees, some a bit straggly, but still healthy and green with no evidence of rot. The garden beds were as she remembered, perhaps less cared for. The compost heap, now larger than previously, had a hole in one side where the composted materials had been shovelled out. Her spirits lifted. Yes, she thought, this place is special. She smiled and turned to Maisie who had seated herself under the veranda. She was surprised to see Maisie's eyes turned up in her head and her arms were spread wide with the palms upwards. There was a big reassuring smile on her face. Wow! Thought Jenny, just like the meditation we used to do up the coast.

After a moment Maisie opened her eyes and said, 'Jenny, the garden loves you and is very happy you've returned. You are the one to have the baby you spoke about as a toddler.'

'How very mystifying,' Jenny said, with a puzzled frown on her face. 'I don't believe in fairies anymore. Maisie, are you feeling okay?'

'I'm fine and I'm sure I don't know about fairies either but didn't Shakespeare say, "... there are more things in heaven and earth, Horatio than are dreamt of in your philosophy?" No matter, the future will unfold. You don't have a partner do you?'

'No, I don't.'

'Then all is well. Let me and the Fairy consider things.'

'Please Maisie, no matchmaking. I am looking for the simple life,' Jenny said with a smile.

'Of course dear.'

With a word in the right ear, Jenny received the job at the Chemist shop and over the months Maisie regularly chatted with her when she was filling her prescriptions. Jenny settled into Burravale and her new house and with Maisie's encouragement, started her own garden. On her days off, she would often meet Maisie, sometimes at the old house to help with the garden or sometimes at Maisie's home for a cup of tea.

Two years after Jenny's arrival, Maisie was at the old house dozing under the veranda at the end of her meditation. There arose in her mind an unusually stark image; nothing like she normally encountered when snoozing. She saw a hunted young soul fleeing along the roads and across the paddocks towards the safe citadel of Burravale from which emanated a blue glow. In her dream, he was exhausted and though his body was strong, his armour was dented and broken from battles and defeats. There were bandaged wounds on his head and his enemies were gaining ground. Suddenly a protective blue force leapt out from the citadel to hide him. The pursuers stopped, confused.

The Fairy floated into the dream and pointed to the young knight. Maisie heard the words, 'He is wounded and sick in the mind, Maisie. Give him a roof over his head because we need this man. And you and I will have our very, very special grandson.'

Maisie smiled and nodded. *Yes, that's how it will be.*

Anne Foggo

Anne-Marie Foggo spent her formative years in country South Oz. Writes both poetry and prose. Enjoys the challenge of finding the perfect words, to express feelings and paint pictures of the world around us and in which she grew up.

The Crow

Bleak winter days of dullness.
A crow's presence on a limb.
Embodiment of sadness,
as the weather closes in.

Glistening like black satin.
Evoking evil by sight.
Like the fiend Satan
winging through in flight.

Spiritual sign of the dead
linking life with nether world.
Dark omen of grim dread.
What does it herald?

Anne Foggo

Travis James

Travis James is a retired manager and technical writer, having written two instruction manuals for the Australian Navy and many work instruction procedures for Industry. He has completed two novels of his trilogy and is working on the concluding novel. As a member of the Marion Writers group he has written many short stories.

Animal lives

The headlines on the screen read:

'Animal Lives admits "losing" three people over the last six months. At the coronial inquiry into the death of an animal induced scientist in February last year, the directors of the company acknowledged three animals induced with the minds of people did not return to agreed pick up points over the last six months. But the Company denies they have lost the people as the bodies are now in the local hospital. The Company refuses to supply their books to verify this number. The Company refuses to accept the absence of a personality in the bodies signifies the death of the person. Neurological scientists are due to be called to give evidence tomorrow. Other Animal Induction franchises have been called to give evidence but have so far refused to attend the hearing....'

Charlie, sat there and read the headlines, perhaps he should make them more dramatic, like 'Animal Lives losing people each month' or 'Animal Induction agencies losing people at unprecedented rate'. No he couldn't print that, although it was beginning to look as though a lot more people had been lost than first reported. He closed his eyes and tried to image what it would be like to be inducted in to an animal. What would it feel like? What type of animal would he like? He wondered if the paper would fund a couple of weeks as a bird. Perhaps an eagle? He imagined soaring though the heavens, flying low across the fields and then high into the sky.

Charlie and the company lawyers signed the contract. The news-paper's lawyers were not happy about the indemnity clauses but conceded if he was going to be induced into an animal then the contract had to be signed.

With the medical check out of the way he was led into what looked like a surgical suite. A helmet with a cable which led to a computer had been fitted over his head. On a bed next to him lay a wedge tailed eagle. Its head was covered by a smaller, but similar helmet.

'When you wake, you'll feel a whole lot different. Don't try to move the anaesthetic is rather strong and it makes moving very difficult for some time. You won't be able to move your wings as we'll have them tied to your body.' The nurse looked rather bored and somewhat disinterested in the proceedings. 'When you're fully recovered we'll take you outside so you can stretch your wings and when you're ready you can fly away. But do remember, you must come back here in fourteen days. We'll implant a little timer in your memory, so when it tells you, come back straight away. Now relax while we administer the drugs.

Blackness, the feeling of being tied down, he couldn't move. Noises, everywhere noises, he knew he should be able to recognise some of them but there were other's he didn't recognise. His wings and legs were bound, a wave of panic swept through his bird-body, everything was coming in to focus. He could see people moving about; some of the noises appeared to be coming from their mouths but his bird-mind wasn't adapted to recognising speech.

One was coming towards him, he tried to escape but the bindings were too tight. The person stroked his head, he tried to snap at the hand but the thing on his head restricted his movement. He was moving he could feel the bumps in the surface as they wheeled him in to another room. He could smell other animals. Hands lifted him up and put him in a cage. Terror engulfed him – he was in a cage again. Memories of the dart hitting him in the chest and the fall to the ground and then being cooped up in the cage flooded through his bird-mind.

He was awake again, the bindings were gone, and he struggled to his feet. Everything was different; the panicking human-mind fought with the bird-mind. Finally, the anaesthetic cleared allowing the human-mind to meld with the bird-mind. He flapped his wings and walked around the cage. This wasn't too bad, he could control this body, but this body wanted to be out of the cage, to be free. Every so often a human would come by the cage and look at him, but his bird-mind couldn't process what the human was saying. He squawked back but at meaningless sounds. Raw meat was given to him, the taste was sickening to the human-mind but the bird-mind gulped it down.

The new day brought release. He flapped his wings and let the bird-mind take him up into the heavens. He soared high above the land and looked down; the bird-mind found a thermal and rose higher. The view was breath-taking. This was everything he imagined. Down below the houses looked like red squares all set out in neat rows. People were moving dots and cars – multi coloured boxes, hurtled along the black bitumen.

The first day of freedom brought more flying; he just couldn't get enough of it. High over a field the bird-mind told him it was mealtime. The eagle circled over the field as the eyes searched for movement, there! There below a field mouse was being careless. The bird-mind had its prey in sight, he tried to stop the bird-mind, he could imagine what was about to happen. But the bird-mind was in charge; it swooped down, closer and closer until finally the lunge and a struggling mouse in its claws.

His human-mind reeled in horror as the bird-mind took the prey back to a tree and ate. The human-mind wanted to escape the horror, the death screams of the mouse and the taste of the raw flesh. Now Charlie understood why so many people came back from animal inductions a little different. Humans had travelled a long way from this level of brutality.

Charlie was sure that being thrust back to their primordial roots had shaken up so many that they needed therapy to forget their experiences.

The joy of flight was gone, now his sole purpose was to survive for the next thirteen days.

Charlie looked at his salad sandwich, like most people who

had an animal induction he couldn't stand the sight or smell of raw or even cooked meat. The computer screen read,

'My fourteen days as an eagle.
This journalist's terror and wonder as
a wedge tailed eagle'.

He had survived, but every so often the screams and the taste of raw meat would impinge on his mind. How was he going to write this? It was the truth so he could legally write this story but how could he write about the horror, the sheer brutality of what he'd experienced? Families of other lost people had piggy-backed on the coronial inquiry and were now in the process of suing Animal Lives and the other franchises, but the iron clad contracts were making it very hard to get any compensation. One witness at the coronial inquiry had suggested that people were allowing their own minds to dissolve into the animal-mind - a subtle form of suicide, while others argued that a couple had mistakenly chosen migratory animals and birds and were then unable to get back to the designated point on the allotted date. Another witness had stated that one human induced animal was killed and eaten by another animal – the very thought sent a shiver up his spine.

Charlie's newspaper story had caused quite a stir, so much so he had been called to give evidence to the coronial inquest.

Now the public wanted to know more about animal induction.

'Professor Ingsat, welcome to Investigation Nightly,' the woman journalist smiled at the middle-aged man sitting opposite her. 'We have opened up the viewer panel to give our viewers the chance to comment on today's interview.'

Oh great! 'Thank you, ah, – Audrey,' The company lawyers had told him he had to appear and try to hose down the problem of the lost people otherwise he would have told her to piss off. He didn't need this interference in his life. There were still problems with the induction process that needed to be ironed out.

'Professor you invented the induction process, can you tell us how it works.'

'Well, it's a bit complex but it's simply a process of impressing the human psyche on to that of an animal,' It wasn't worth going any deeper, this blond bimbo or the fools out there wouldn't understand the technicalities of suppressing and then over writing the animal's neurons with the human's neural energy.

[#joe432 love 2 b horse]

[#bart659 lion 4 me]

'Surely it's not as simple as that. How do you impress a human's neural energy on an animal's mind?'

He swore under his breath – not another half-educated reporter, 'Well no - of course not. First we have to suppress the animal's neuron activity, then selectively neutralise any ongoing thoughts and memories. Once the brain is, mmm, clear we can then impress the human's activity on to the animal brain.'

[#cic9875 bird brain?]

'But a human mind is so much bigger.'

[#joe432 not much]

[#cic9875 lol]

'But not an elephants – or a dolphin,' he smirked. 'But you have to realise that most of the human mind is taken up with automatic functions and communication. Animals don't speak so we don't have to worry about that.'

'What happens to the animal once the human neural energy is withdrawn?'

'Mmm, I'm not sure, we release the animal, I don't know what happens then.'

'Is the animal able to return to its former life?'

'Yes, we release them and to the best of our knowledge they continue with no problems.'

'Do you think the animal is affected by this – let's say experience?'

'I'm not sure.'

'Has anyone bothered to investigate this?' She had been hoping to sensationalise the lost people but this was another unexpected bonus. The animal libbers would love this.

'No, not to my knowledge.'

[#killo784 animal cruelty]

'You're possibly killing these animals for someone's fun?'

'Ahh – probably – but man's been doing that for eons.'

[#killo784 thought we now know better]

'That doesn't make it right – does it?'

'No but it does make it,' He put his fingers up to imitate quotation marks, "normal."

[#killo784 who for]

'Somehow I don't think the animal liberation people are going to see it quite that way. Could there be some vestige of the human still left in the animal?'

'Mm possibly.'

'Oh let's get back to the people aspect...'

'I wish you would,' He was swearing under his breath – the last thing he wanted was a group of do-gooder animal lovers breathing down his neck.

'I understand that when you lose someone it's the person's consciousness that is lost, the body is still there and on life support?'

'Yes, we take great care of the body, without the consciousness the body will survive by itself but we prefer to monitor it and make sure it is well nourished.'

'So the body would die without food?'

[#cic9875 stupid question]

'Of course!' Of course it would die you bloody idiot.

'How long can you keep a body in that way?'

He hesitated; this could be dangerous – 'Two to three months.'

'And these lost people, how long have they been under your care?'

'Shit,' he thought. 'Not as long as that.'

'Professor as I understand it the first person to get lost was over six months ago, are you still caring for that person's body?'

'No. The body died.'

[#joe433 poor schmuck]

'What happened?'

'I'm not sure I'm not a medical doctor.'

[#cic9875 OMG]

'And you didn't try to find out?" she paused, 'Isn't the current coronial investigation trying to clear up this matter?'

'I've got medical doctors to do that.'

'OK, what going to happen to the bodies of the people you say are lost?'

[#cic9875 feed them to the animals @ zoo]

[#BART659 sick bstd]

'Well, we'll send them to the hospitals.'

'When you say the people are lost what exactly do you mean?'

'Well the person has not returned to their body,' He shrugged his shoulders as though it was only a minor matter.

'How does that happen?'

'The person is supposed to return to the collection point at the allotted time so we un-induct the consciousness from the animal and return it to the body.'

'And if they don't?'

'Oh we go back several times and wait for them.'

'When do you declare a person lost?'

'After six weeks '

'The coronial inquiry is about the death of a Professor Matthews a naturalist, and the inquiry was told he chose to be inducted into a migratory bird. Is that correct?"

'I...I think so.'

Audrey looked at him with surprise, 'I thought you would have known that. - It's also been suggested that if a person selects a migratory bird, then they won't be back until the seasons change – that could be six or even twelve months. Is that correct?'

'Mmm – yes.'

'Would anything happen to the person in that time?'

Ingsat thought for few seconds, 'I suppose the... that there is a good possibility that the person would or could have been overcome by the animal mind.'

'Could you explain please?'

'No it's too difficult to explain.'

'But are you saying that the person would be lost?'

'Ahh yes.'

'Would anything be left?'

'After 12 months – probably not'

'Do you keep the body alive for that length of time?'

'There would be no point.'

'Do you know this for a fact or are you just guessing'

He glared at her, how dare she suggest he would guess. 'What's your name...oh yes Audrey, I do not guess! We have computer models that predict the decay of the human energy within the animal mind.'

'If that is the case why did you allow Professor Matthews to be inducted on to a migratory bird?'

She watched with more than a little satisfaction as he squirmed in his chair but he did not answer.

'Just to swap things around, you've already stated that one body in your care has died. What would happen if that happened before the animal returned? What would you do with the person in the animal?'

[#cic9875atta girl]

He simply looked at her with a weird blank look on his face.

[#joe432 he don't know]

'Professor what would happen?'

'Ahh it's not important – let's move on.'

'Oh to change track, it's quite expensive to be inducted in to an animal?'

'Yes – but I'm not prepared to discuss costs on the television.'

'Why not?'

'It's between the client and Animal Lives, and depends upon the type of animal is selected.'

Audrey paused to allow the viewers to absorb this, 'What types of animals are selected.'

'Oh we've had several lions, elephants, cheetahs a lot of people like eagles – I guess it's the freedom to be able to fly,' he paused for several seconds, 'We've even had a couple of seals. They're the ones I know about at Animal Lives, other franchises may have other animals.'

[#joe432 elephant 4 me]

'You've made a lot of money though animal Induction?'

[#cic9875 all in the $]

He thought about the new Ferrari sitting in the TV station car park, 'Yes I have.'

'Professor, you've experienced induction, can you tell us what it was like?'

He broke out in a cold sweat, 'Oh – oh it was a... a g-great experience, I went in to a lion...' the sweating got worse. As the camera moved in for a close up showing the perspiration beading on his face, 'It was - very - ah - interesting.' The beading was getting worse.

'Professor, isn't correct that you had several months of deep psychoanalyst after your return?'

But there was no answer.

'What upset you so much professor?'

'The lion made a k - kill,' He stammered as he stood and ran towards the studio door but half-way there he vomited.

[#cic9875 couldn't take own ind lol]

Mars Drilling

Vizier-Is walked into the library and looked around. The walls are covered by shelves crammed full of data storage capsules. He remembered his childlike amazement when, as a newly appointed Vizier, the Reader had taught him how to use a reading machine. The Reader had told him he didn't expect him, as the new Vizier, to ever need to use the library. That's what the Readers are for. They are the specialists in data retrieval and in analysing facts.

There were two working machines then and he had secretly promised himself he would learn everything in the library, but that was many, many rotations ago. But as the settlement governor he had had too much to do to fore fill his dream.

Now standing here he wished he had followed his dream. Perhaps he could have been a better governor. Perhaps he would know how to handle this problem.

He walked through to the reading machine room.

'Reader-Ve, can you hear that noise?'

Reader-Ve was sitting at the last, working, reading machine. He nodded his head. 'The Western Settlement heard it too.' He said, without looking up from the screen.

'When?'

'Oh about twenty rotations ago. They told me they detected it several rotations before that in the Western end of the Basin.' Reader-Ve still didn't look up from the machine; the Vizier was interrupting his concentration. His mind was grappling with the surprising suggestion— that they once lived on the surface. No, that couldn't be true; they had always lived in underground settlements.

'Why didn't you tell me?' Vizier-Is asked.

'Didn't think it was worth the effort, I'm busy with this research. I found a ...'

'I've been trying to contact the Vizier in the Western Settlement but can't get through, do you know of any problems?'

The Reader didn't answer.

'Reader, don't ignore me. Do you know of any problems?'

Still no answer

'Reader, is it possible the com-link is not working?' Perhaps it was like everything else in this settlement. "No longer working". Most of the machines had failed; they were down to half food rations and somewhere there was an air monitor that someone had turned off because the beeping had turned into a constant scream.

'We could send someone to the Western Settlement to find what is happening.'

'What? How?' Vizier-Is took a mental step back—he'd not known this was possible.

'Use the tunnel. People used to travel back and forth between the settlements many rotations ago.'

'Why didn't you say so?'

'No one asked.' The Reader was still looking at the screen.

'Why don't we do it now?'

The Reader continued to look at the screen.

'Reader, turn and face me.'

With a moan the reader swivelled his chair to face the Vizier, 'There was some sort of dispute so the two settlements decided to seal the doors.'

'Can we reopen the doors?'

'Probably.'

'Where are they?'

'Don't know.' The Reader was getting really annoyed; he turned back to the reading machine.

'READER, will you stop this infernal investigation about our history and start to do your job? What is this noise we can hear and where is the door and while I'm at it, will you give the maintenance people the information they need to repair the food machines?'

Reader-Ve shrugged his shoulders.

'I want the answers by the next rotation.' Vizier-Is was getting annoyed.

'Can I remind you, Vizier-Is, I'm allowed to look at whatever I please.'

'Yes—when there is nothing else to do. NOW we have three problems that must take precedence over your investigation. Tell me if this noise is dangerous and where the tunnel doors are and when you have done that give the maintenance people the information they need.'

'There's only one door this end.'

Vizier-Is bent down so his mouth was close to the reader's ear, 'DO as I command! You have one rotation.'

"Or what? I'm the only one who can use the reading machines." The reader thought to himself as the Vizier left the room. I was right in not teaching anybody else how to use the reading machines; I have complete control over them. He looked over at the pile of notes he had printed for the repair of food machines and inwardly laughed. "When I'm ready."

'Reader, what have you found out about the noise? And the door?'

'The door is in room JU-23'

'And the noise? It's getting closer to us. And I still can't contact the Western Settlement.'

Another shrug by the Reader.

'Reader-Ve you must investigate. I command you!'

'Why?'

'We need to find out what it is and if it's going to harm the settlement.'

The reader continued to stare at the machine.

'As the Vizier I demand you investigate.'

'Perhaps there is something in the records?'

'Reader-Ve, investigate the noise!' He shouted before turning and storming out of the library. "I don't know why I allow him to spend all his time in there, what has he achieved – nothing! He was supposed to help the maintenance people fix the other reading machines and the food machine—oh there were so many machines that don't work and now I can't contact the Western

Settlement."

'Reader-Ve, you were ordered to investigate the noise, but you haven't moved out of the library. What have you done?'

'There are many references to a noise that moves around. It could be one of the shakes, but it doesn't have the vibration like a shake. The capsules talk of something they call wind that makes a long noise that moves around. There are very old references to things called flyers that make a noise that moves across the sky. Some machinery makes a noise that lasts a long time but that is generally stationary. I found references to musical instruments that make noises and something called a drum—there are so many sources of noise...'

'Reader-Ve, what is it, what can you tell us? Is it dangerous?'

'Or it could be something called thunder that appears to move around. There are many references to thunder...'

'Do you have any idea what is happening?' Vizier-Is was fed-up with Reader-Ve's meandering.

'You're the last of the Reader's. We don't have anyone else who can read these texts.'

Reader-Ve was enjoying the power he held over the Vizier. He should be the governor, not that idiot.

'Maybe it's a machine in another settlement starting up, or it...'

Vizier-Is slammed his fist down on the table. 'You are going to kill us all. If that other machine was working I'd sit down myself and investigate.'

"That's why it's not working." Reader-Ve thought.

Vizier-Is stormed out of the library again. On the way a

maintenance technician approached him to say they had located the new source of the sound—it was directly above one of the machine rooms.

Together they walked to the room and looked up. The room was beginning to vibrate. As they watched the ceiling began to crack and a large piece fell to the ground. A rotating shaft slowly pushed its way into the room. It slowly moved down. It didn't stop when it hit the top of a machine but slowly crushed the machine into the ground. Having bored its way through the machine, the shaft continued down into the floor and kept going.

'Vizier-Is, what is it?' The maintenance technician asked.

'I have no idea.'

'Can the Reader help us?'

Vizier-Is looked at the technician and then back at the rotating shaft, 'No he's...' then a horrible thought struck him. They were doomed. Reader-Ve has lost his ability to become concerned with anything other than his research. When he dies there will be no one left to read the capsules and answer questions.

'What does that machine do? Is it important?' Vizier-Is asked.

The maintenance technician, too fixated on the rotating shaft to speak, simply shook his head.

'Get an Operator, we need to know.' Vizier-Is stood watching the shaft rotate as it slowly worked its way further into the floor.

'Vizier-Is you called? ... What is that?' The Operator asked, staring at the crushed machine and the rotating shaft.

'I don't know, is that machine important?'

'No – it's never worked.'

The three stood transfixed as the shaft stopped rotating for several seconds and then began to rotate in the opposite direction as it slowly worked its way upwards. The shaft pulled the top off the crushed machine. The now separated top began to spin with the rotating shaft as it was dragged towards the ceiling. When it struck the ceiling it was pushed along the shaft and finally fell to the floor.

For several minutes the three stood and listened as the shaft worked its way up the hole it had bored.

Then a whooshing sound started as the air in the cavern began to escape out through the bore hole.

'Vizier-Is, what do we do?' The Operator asked.

'We need to cover the hole.'

'But we can't reach it. How do we do that? What do we use?' The maintenance technician asked in terror.

In a terrifying moment of clarity he realised he was witnessing the destruction of his settlement. We can't even fix up a hole in the ceiling.

'Ken look at this,' Dave was standing over the core slicing bench staring at what appeared to be a coloured thread sticking out of the metallic coloured aggregate between two pieces of rock.

Ken carefully pulled it out 'Looks like piece of wire. But where did it come from?' He commented as he walked over to the microscope.

'There's some sort of plastic here.' Dave said, pulling a piece of blue material out of the same section of soil.

'How far down did you say this was?' Ken asked.

'About thirty meters, the drill hit something very hard and then nothing before it hit another hard barrier.'

'This isn't rock.' Ken had pulled the piece of rock out from above the aggregate. With practiced care he brushed the soil away and took it over to a microscope for a closer look.

'Not any natural rock I've ever seen.

'At a guess I'd say it's a form of concrete, but it's completely homogenous. There's no grain or any form of structure—plastic?'

'What in hell did we hit?'

'Dave, didn't you say that gas blew out of the hole when you pulled the drill out.'

'Yeh. It was still outgassing when we left. Same...as the other one where we hit a hard barrier.' the blood drained from his face, 'What have we done?'

'Let's look at the other sample. What number was it?'

'Ah...Here it is.' He pulled the core sample out of the rack and took it over to the cutting table.

Minutes later he had the sample sliced in two.

The two men looked for the same rock near the bottom of the core.

'It looks like the same concrete structure, but there's only one here.'

Ken slowly prised the piece of concrete out of the soil, but when he had it out it came apart to form two semicircular disks.'There's two here, they look exactly alike. Are there two or only one there?'

'No there's another here.'

'I'll go down to the material guys to see if they can recognise it' Ken said, as he walked out of the door.

Dave scooped out the metallic aggregate that was in between the rock disks. He cleared a space on the examination table and slowly spread the aggregate out. 'This isn't soil, looks, more of that wire, and this...' he said forgetting Ken had left the room. He reached for the phone and dialled a number.

'Sam, you got a minute?' He stood there looking at the debris spread across the table, too stunned to say anything.

The door swung open and Sam the electronics specialist walked in. 'Got a problem? She put her tool bag down on Dave's writing desk and walked up next to him. 'What are you looking at there?'

'What would you say this is?' he asked, looking at the debris on the table.

She poked around a bit and picked up what appeared to be a shattered piece of grainy plastic and walked over to the microscope, 'Whose computer did you smash this time?'

Dave was now standing next to her, 'Computer?'

'Yes, this is a circuit board, although I've never seen anything like this, but it's definitely a circuit of some description.' When she saw the look on his face she frowned.

'It was at the bottom of a drill sample.'

'But that means...,' she walked back to the debris and selected several other samples which she put one at a time, under the microscope. 'I don't recognise half of these components but they are definitely some form of electronics.'

She turned from the microscope and faced David. 'Do you

think they're still alive?'

'Not anymore, the hole outgassed when we pulled out the drill. If they were alive, we killed them.'

Mars explorers kill Martians

Scientists drilling for soil core samples in the Placid Sea Basin appear to have broken into subterranean caverns containing equipment. Bore-hole photos show rooms with equipment similar to that used on earth. One photo shows what appears to be part of a body. All drilling has ceased until NASA has considered their next move. UN has ordered a complete review of activity on Mars.

Detailed photographic explorations of the caverns prove they were the domain of an intelligent species. While the function of the equipment could only be guessed at, the fact it exists proves beyond doubt intelligent beings once inhabited the caverns. A ground penetrating radar unit was used to explore the Placid Sea basin. Three caverns were identified; two where the drills had taken samples. Meanwhile NASA and the UN tried to work their way through the complexity of having discovered intelligent life on Mars and finding out who was responsible for the deaths of the beings in the two caverns. Some churches and newly formed Save-the-Martians groups demanded the colony pack up and come home. Other churches and certain countries branded the report a lie by NASA in order to get increased funding. The very fact that life, that appeared to be intelligent, was discovered on another planet was causing untold discussion.

Commander Stalovich called the meeting to order. All the colonists were there. 'We've been able to analyse the remnants of the atmosphere that remains in the Eastern cavern. While it appears to be very high in carbon dioxide it's not unlike ours. We're testing for biological agents now but nothing appears to be there.'

'Could we breathe it?' one of the staff asked.

'Not with so much CO2 but otherwise yes. But I wouldn't until we know about any biological agents in the air.'

'Do we know what they looked like?' One of the women asked.

'No, we only have a partial shot of what looks like a body. We are only assuming the being was alive before we broke through the ceiling. For all we know it could have been dead for centuries.' He shrugged his shoulders.

'Is the body decaying?' another asked

'Not that we can see, but we can only see a small section of what appears to be a foot.'

'Ok, let's get back to basics,' Commander Stalovich said, 'we know there are three caverns, and two of these were occupied. So it's a fair assumption that the third one is as well.' He held up his hand with four fingers pointing up, 'Do we try to communicate,' he ticked off one finger, 'If so how?' He ticked off another finger, 'are there any more caverns?' Another finger, 'What do we do now? Do we limit ourselves to surface exploration and wait for someone else to make the decisions or what?' He bent the final finger.

'I have been looking at the Placid Sea basin and I think the

Sea of Rocks is very similar. I'm wondering if there are other caverns there.' Dave said. 'I'd like to do a ground radar scan on the basin.'

'What makes you think they would be there?' Stalovich asked.

'Both basins are near the North Pole and that means a supply of water. Both are in what appears to have been deep valleys that have filled with soil and they are relatively close to one another.'

'I did a high frequency magnetic scan between the three settlements in the Placid Basin and there are strong indications there are power lines or communications links between them. So if these are communication links or power lines then there could be similar links between the Placid Sea basin and the Sea of Rocks basin. We should be able to find other caverns very quickly.' Sam offered to the discussion.

'Just follow the bouncing ball or in this case, humming cable.' Another person quipped.

'Ok, follow on Sam's suggestion.' Stalovich decided, looking at Dave.

'No caverns were found in the Sea of Rocks basin but there appears to be two in the Anderson Basin. We found where the cables went over the mountains. The UV and sand have done a lot of damage so we did our best to provide extra covering and covered them with more soil. One of the Anderson caverns is very large and is radiating a lot of magnetic noise, so I'm suggesting there is a lot of equipment functioning down there.' Dave reported

'Any idea how many inhab...beings?' Stalovich asked.

'No way to tell, but the communications between the two

Anderson caverns fluctuates a lot indicating it's possibly human, oops, Martian driven. We also put a receiver in the ground next to the cable. There was a change in data rate as soon as we buried it. I wonder if this is normal or we disturbed something.'

'Any hope of understanding it?' someone asked, referring to the data being transmitted along the cable.

'No, not at this stage.'

'That makes five caverns. Any chance of there being others?' the commander asked.

'We detected two links radiating away from the large cavern in the Anderson cavern so I'd suggest at least two more. But we haven't had time to investigate these.'

'Where does the power come from?'

'While we were tracking the link between the two Anderson caverns the magnetic field slowly declined and then reversed, suggesting they each generate their own power but also share it between the caverns.' Sam answered.

'The next supply satellite is due here is five days, provided it doesn't crash like the last one.'

'Great I'm running out face cream.' Ann commented, trying to make light of a difficult situation.

The others giggled, but they all understood they needed the food the satellite was bringing. The colony had been on food rationing since the last satellite exploded on its approach to Mars.

'The satellite's exploded.'

'Just like the last one. Now what do we do?'

'I've contacted Earth. They'll do their best to get one away but it will take a couple of months. But first we need to work out why both satellites exploded at the same point in space.'

'They shot it down,' said Sam.

'Who, the Martians?'

'Yes, there was a large power spike immediately before the satellite exploded. I'd say there is a gun or something protecting Mars from meteorites.'

'Can we work out where it is and disable it?'

'Shouldn't be too hard, we know the direction the satellite was coming in from so we know what area of Mars was pointed towards the satellite.'

'You sure it was a terrain mounted gun?'

'N...no.'

'OK, get on with it. We need the next supply satellite to land.' He looked at Ann and smiled, 'Sorry about your face cream.'

She smiled but mouthed the word 'Bastard'.

'Seepar, the protector has fired again.' The settlement chief looked at his chief scientist with a quizzical look.

'It's the second time it's fired in two hundred and sixty rotations.'

'But it could be...'

'The protectors haven't fired in over thirty thousand rotations and now twice in two hundred and sixty rotations and at the same point in space. Something strange is happening. Remember, we've lost contact with two of our settlements.'

'Could it simply be the com-links are down?'

'No, we can test them, the machinery at both ends is working correctly, but no one is answering. There is one puzzling thing; the air monitors in both settlements are registering no air.'

'Could they have been hit by a quake?'

'No, we would have registered anything that big.'

'We know that both settlements were deteriorating but both at the same time?'

'Commander we've found the gun, but neutralising it is going to be difficult.'

'Why?'

'It's the size of a mountain. There are, what we would call arrays, buried just under the soil all over the mountain. Our best theory is that they discharge in a sequence to get the angle to hit the incoming object.'

'Would that cover all of Mars?'

'No, our guess is there's one at the Southern pole.'

'How do we stop it destroying the satellite?'

'There's something peculiar about the placement. The arrangement leaves a dead zone directly above each pole.' Another of the investigating team added.

'Is there any way we can test that?'

'No we'd need something the size of the satellites travelling at the same speed.'

'Do we know that size and speed are factors?'

'If we assume it's an automatic meteor defence system, only meteors of a certain size and travelling above a certain speed would cause enough damage to warrant the energy expenditure.'

'But you have to remember that we've been sending probes

to Mars for years and this is the first time the gun has activated. Do they know we are here?'

'What? After we destroyed two of their caverns—I'd say they are well aware we're here.'

'Remember the supply satellites are larger and travel much faster than any of the probes. Size and speed could be factors.' The one woman in the investigation team added to the conversation. 'Could we slow the satellite down before it reaches Mars so it comes in slower?'

'So they may not know we are here?'

'They know we're here but if we are dealing with an automatic system...' She became lost in her thoughts about other possibilities.

'What about the hole at the poles?' the commander asked.

'That is only supposition based on the fact we haven't found any way for the guns to aim in that direction.'

'Ok, so you're all saying that speed is an important factor?'

Most of the team nodded.

'Any factors we haven't considered?'

Not getting any comments, Stalovich said, 'I'll contact NASA and get them to slow the satellite down.'

'While we wait for the satellite have a look at the poles, could there be a reason why the guns don't point there?'

'Commander, the satellite is approaching what we believe to be the gun boundary.'

The entire Mars contingent was crowded into the communication room. Sam sat at the console.

'Thirty minutes to where the last two satellites were

destroyed.' Her radar screen was picking up the blip of the satellite, as it hurtled towards Mars. 'NASA was only able to reduce the speed by eleven per cent. Here's hoping that was enough.'

Everyone stood silently, their eyes fixed on the monitor.

'Twenty minutes.'

The tension in the room was palpable.

'Ten minutes.'

'Five minutes.'

'Four minutes.'

'Three minutes, no build up in line current'

'Shit the current's building up.'

'No.'

'My god, no.' a woman murmured.

'Two minutes.'

'One minute.'

'Line current has dropped,' she was sweating, 'that's strange.'

'On limit.'

'One minute pass limit.'

'Thank you.' Someone said in the background.

'Don't be too eager. We don't know how these guns work.'

'Two minutes pass limit.'

No one relaxed until the satellite had landed. 'Hope you guys are up for a long drive it's landed a hundred click's from here.' Sam quietly announced.

'As long as it's in one piece,' came from the back of the room.

'Seepar, the protectors nearly fired in the last rotation. I was at the console and decided that the meteor or whatever it was wasn't going fast enough to do any damage and it was heading away from the settlements so I cancelled the firing. An interesting fact, it was slowing down.'

The Settlement Chief looked at his Chief Scientist with a concerned look. 'Shouldn't the meteor be accelerating?'

The chief scientist nodded, 'That would have been the third time in the last four hundred rotations. All coming from the same direction in space.'

'What's happening?'

'I'm going to train a couple of our people to take one of the flyers out to the crash site to have a look at what hit us.'

Two days later the colony had an impromptu celebration, the dried rations never tasted so good.

'What did you find on the pole photos?'

'Not a lot, but the quality is strangely lacking, it almost seems as though something is blurring the image. I've programmed the terrain satellite to do a fly-over and take photos from different angles.'

'Commander, have a look at these photos.' He spread them out on the conference table. 'Here are the perpendicular photos of the North Pole; see how they appear fuzzy in this area.' He circled an area around the North Pole with his finger.

The commander nodded.

'Here, from almost directly above the poles, the fuzziness is gone and there appears to be a small but deep depression.'

'Do you think something is being hidden?'

'Maybe, but it could be another mechanism, perhaps some form of shield, that could be why the guns don't need to point over the poles.'

'Seepar, some sort of container landed. It must have come in very quickly because the outer skin is burnt. Going by the tracks, a ground vehicle drove up to it and also, going by what appears to be footprints, they unloaded what was in it and drove away. Our flyer didn't have the range to follow the tracks very far. We are in the process of recovering the thing that landed.' The Chief Scientist had sat himself down at the Chief's desk. "Mm it appears they are bipeds'

'Are you telling me there are other...?' Pictures of ghastly two legged creatures from childhood stories haunted his mind.

The Chief Scientist nodded.

'What do we do?' The Settlement Chief said, sitting back in his couch. 'Could they have destroyed the two settlements?'

'No idea, but the coincidence?'

The Chief Scientist walked into the Settlement Chief's office and closed the door. 'The Eastern Settlement has told me they know where these things are. They are within striking distance.'

'Give them all the energy they need.'

NNNNNOOOOO!

'Well then, it's decided. We'll demolish the Arcade and have Global build the car park!' The Mayor sat down, and let out a sigh of relief. It had been a long hard battle but he'd won—he had fulfilled his side of the bargain. Thoughts of a new holiday home floated through his mind.

'NNNNNOOOOO,' rumbled through the council chambers.

'An earthquake!' someone shouted.

'We don't have them here,' another councillor shouted, looking towards the door.

'Sounded like someone was saying "No".' The Speaker was too scared to add she thought it was the building; she couldn't stand more ridicule from the Mayor and the other males in the room.

'It was an earthquake,' the Mayor responded. 'Tomorrow I'll have the contract signed so Global can start.'

'NNNNNOOOOO,' rumbled again. Glasses toppled, spilling water over paperwork while books slid off tables the floor.

'Shit, what's happening,' yelled the normally un-flappable

mayoral personal assistant, 'that was definitely a "No".'

'Crap! That was an earthquake,' the mayor said, but not quite as loud as before.

One if the councillors sat back and thought about it—the mayor had been doing his best to bulldoze the demolition proposal through council for the last six months. It was well known he had friends in Global. How much was the Mayor was pocketing from this little exercise. No one wanted the Arcade to go, it was the last of the original buildings in the city—it could be refurbished, after all it was heritage listed. But then that could easily be side stepped if the right palm was greased with enough money.

He wondered if the buildings themselves wanted the Arcade kept. Could they be fighting back? Was it possible?

He walked over to a window and looked down to see the Mayor's car parked on the other side of the street. Directly above it, a large section of concrete façade was loose, if it fell.... Perhaps he should warn the Mayor but then maybe the buildings should be allowed to cast the last, deciding vote.

The Longing

I have a longing, one that has been with me since that day in the market in Denpasar, so long ago. It's an ache in my chest. It feels as though someone reached in, grabbed my heart and ripped it out.

The father, war weary and looking to escape the horrors of war, ventured into the market and saw me standing there, bare breasted holding a water pitcher on my head. There were many of us there on the day; we were doing all the things good women do in Bali. Some were cooking, others were simply walking and two of us were nursing babies. But he fell in love with me at first sight. What was it that made him buy me? Was it the way I stood so tall, or perhaps the slightly disconcerting look on my face? I will never know, he never told me.

Home from the war, the father poured his energies into establishing the family home, working and raising two children. Not once did he care for me or even ask about the ache in my chest. He was simply too busy. Each week his wife would dust me with not so much as a kind word or even a thought about who I was. She never knew about the longing that ached in my chest.

The father is gone now, leaving me to stand on a small table in the lounge of the family home. But things never stay the same; the wife moved to a smaller place, one she can manage. She puts me on the mantel piece above the heater. As she does there's a faint memory of her husband giving me to her and telling her where he bought me. But he was never able to talk about the war.

The wife has passed on, and the son has purchased the unit. Now I sit on his sideboard and watch the evolving renovation of the home. He sometimes wonders if I was a single woman or a combination of all the women the artist knew. Perhaps I was the artist's wife, or daughter or even his mistress or I may have just been the personification of his ideal woman. Guests come and go but none see me. If they do, I don't rate a comment. It would be nice to feel as though I matter.

The son occasionally sits at the book covered dining table, he spends time working there. He looks at me and wonders. He treasures me, not for who I am, but for the skill of the carver and the connection I had with his father. But the longing goes on. You see I grew as a tall straight tree in the tropical forest on Sulawesi.

Luke's change of heart

Luke stepped off the plane. He took one breath, the same stifling hot air! The same dry red earth and the same spindly gums along the airport boundary. His heart dropped in his chest. Oh, how he hated this place. He started to retrace the events that led up to that night, but his meandering was interrupted by a shout to get on the bus for the trip to the town. No one talked much on the bus, having a priest amongst them tempered their language. But Luke thought only of that night.

As the bus drove down what the locals jokingly called Main Street, he realised Goodawan hadn't changed in all the years. The same rusty, galvanised iron houses spread randomly, although now they were covered with a much thicker layer of dirt. He still hated everything about this town. He groaned inwardly. At least the miner's camp had some semblance of life; even it was centred on the bar in the cafeteria. He remembered some of the movies they watched, most of them DVDs people had copied while they were on leave - even the one's he wasn't supposed to watch.

He got off the bus at the small galvanised shed with "General Store" painted in flaking red letters across the front. Sally worked there after school. He went to walk in but something held him back, would her parents remember him – what would they say? No, he couldn't do it. He turned and walked towards the cemetery. After all this was the only reason he travelled all the way from Perth; there was nothing else he wanted to see. He didn't know where the other lads he was with that night had gone, like most people in his life they just walked away leaving him to face the shit. His father hadn't contacted him since the trial; in one of her rare letters Mum had said Dad had hooked up with the schoolteacher and followed her to her next posting. There she is - a simple grave. The headstone stood up right in the glaring sunlight, 'Sally Robertson, Born 2nd July, 1997 - cruelly taken - 31st March 2014.' He dropped to his knees and buried his face in his hands as the events leading up to that night rampaged through his mind.

'I won't get into any more trouble with the guys.' Luke pleaded, but his father had made up his mind. He knew what Luke's friends were like, always in trouble. Mum and Dad had argued for nearly an hour before Mum slapped Dad across the face and called him a heartless bastard. Dad stood up. 'He's coming with me – that's final.' He turned to Luke. 'Get your gear together; we're going to Goodawan.'

Luke stood up to argue but one look at his father's face told him that it would only result in a slap.

'David you can't take him to Goodawan, all his friends are here,' his Mum pleaded.

'Yeh and look at them, Greg's in jail for stealing a car and two of the others have police records. No, I won't have Luke hanging around with them.' He turned to Luke. 'Get your gear together we're leaving in fifteen minutes.'

Luke hobbled out of the room, swearing under his breath, the moon-boot made walking difficult.

'If you'd been home more this wouldn't have happened.' Mum was crying she didn't want her son stuck out in the middle of the desert.

'You knew I was a geologist when we married. I told you I'd be spending large amounts of time away from the city but you refused to join me. You certainly didn't complain about the money I sent home.'

'What will Luke do in that hole?'

'For one thing he'll be away from those shit-heads and another he'll get an education, there's a company school in Goodawan. I know the schoolteacher.'

'I bet you do.'

'At least she's got an education, unlike that stone-head you hang out with. What's he ride now? A Kawasaki or a Yamaha?' Not looking away from his wife, he raised his voice, 'Luke hurry up we're leaving.'

Luke and his father didn't say more than three worlds on the trip to Goodawan. Even now six months later they rarely spoke even when his father was home from his field trips. Looking out of his bedroom window at spindly gums growing in the dry brown earth between the miner's cabins, Luke repeated the same mantra. I hate this town, I hate the school, I hate the people, I hate tennis, I hate cricket, and I hate everything here.

He slammed his fist down on his knee. He let out a string of obscenities; the once fractured bone was still tender. I hate Dad for making me come to this shit-hole. I hate Mum for allowing him to take me. He sighed. I miss Greg and the guys. His memory swung back to the last time he saw them and the car ride that ended with the stolen car wrapped around a tree. Luke's leg still ached from the break. I hate this shit-hole, I hate this house and I hate it when the schoolteacher visits Dad and tells him how I'm going at school. I hate the school. Then his mind wandered to Sally. She had tanned skin and a slim face. She wasn't like the others, most of whom had been brought up on farms; like him she'd been raised in the Sydney. They would sit through their lunch break discussing all the places they'd been to in Sydney. He liked the way she smiled at him. A warm glow spread through his body when he thought about her.

It was the town dance in two weeks' time. Three times he tried to ask her, but each time his courage failed him. What was stopping him? Why couldn't he ask her while they were at lunch? Now two days before the dance, Roy, the Mine Manager's son, spent the whole day boasting how he was taking Sally to the dance and he was going to make sure he got his just rewards after. Luke fumed. He wanted to punch Roy but he was already on report, one more problem and he'd be dragged before the Mine Manager - his father could lose his job.

The mining camp cafeteria had been cleaned out, given the once over by the camp women and it now hosted the dance. There weren't many women, the few who were at the dance were from either local farms or were living in the camp with their husbands. Sally's parents who ran the General Store had shipped in special decorations and party food for the dance.

Roy put on a sickening Cheshire cat smile when he saw Luke watching him escort Sally in to the dance, but she looked at Luke and sort of smiled and frowned at the same time. Several times during the night when Roy and Sally were in plain sight of Luke, he saw Roy look at him and accidently-on-purpose brush his hands across Sally's breasts. While Luke couldn't hear what Sally said, he could see by her face she wasn't impressed by Roy's behaviour. Roy was obviously boasting to Luke that it was he who was dancing with Sally, not Luke.

Luke and the other boys plonked themselves down at a table in one corner of the cafeteria, well away from the single miners who were doing their best to get drunk. The boys had tried to sit with them but had been told in no uncertain terms to piss off; this was a man's table. Things were very boring for the boys until the barman felt sorry for them and with the mine security personnel having the night off, gave each of them an alcopop drink – the drink the city kids got drunk on. He was suddenly their best friend, so much so that he made several trips to the boy's table through the night.

Luke couldn't take his eyes of Sally and each time Roy got too close his anger rose. He hated every time he saw Roy holding Sally. He hated it when she laughed and smiled at Roy. As the evening crept by the boys got progressively drunk.

There was a crash followed by slurred swearing which was followed by a roar of laughter from his companions as a miner tried to get to his feet. He stumbled across the floor, narrowly missing seated couples on his way to the men's toilet. Minutes later the idea caught on and several other very drunk miners barged their way through the tables towards the toilets. The boys howled with laughter as one of the men missed the doorway and bounced off the wall. Several of the nearby women made degrading comments, but many of them were noticeably unsteady when they went to the Ladies'.

The boys returned to watching the couples dance. 'Shit this is boring, I think I'll go and watch a video.' Andrew commented downing the last of his Strawberry Surprise

'I've g-got an n-new copy o' T-T-Transformers, want to play that?' Peter suggested.

'Let's have some real fun,' Andrew slurred. 'I know where dad keeps the key to the company lockup.'

The boys trooped out leaving the others to their fun. Luke looked back just as Roy tried to kiss Sally but someone stepped in front of Luke so he didn't see her push him away. A short car drive later Andrew disappeared in to his home and minutes later he ran out holding something on a chain. 'Go around the back of the compound, we can get in there.' He said as he climbed back in the car. With the car lights off the car crept around the compound to the spot pointed out by Andrew. Under his instructions the four climbed under the fence and worked their way over to the explosives lockup. Andrew used the key and opened the door just wide enough to slip though.

Minutes later he reappeared with a bundle of short, paper wrapped sticks in his arm. 'Got the fuses in me pocket.' He whispered as the four scampered back to the fence and then the car.

'Whata' we gonna do wit' the dynamite Andrew?' Billy asked. He wasn't the brightest even when he was sober.

This stopped Andrew in his steps. He hadn't thought that far ahead. 'Ahh lets go over to the old mine and let a couple off.'

'Yeh that s-s sounds f-fun.' Stammered Peter.

'Better go to the old entrance so they won't hear the stuff going off.' Added Andrew.

'W-we c-c-can demolish t-the old t-t-tower for t-them,' said Peter.

Andrew taped sticks of dynamite to each of the tower legs, joined the fuses, twisted the ends together and lit the fuse. 'Run' he shouted as he ran for the nearest tailings heap.

The fours sticks blew equal pieces out of each of the tower legs. The effect was the tower simply moved down a couple of meters but stayed upright. 'Ahh shit.' Billy yelled. He'd been looking forward to seeing the tower fall over and shatter on the ground.

'This is no fun,' Luke said 'Gimme one.'

'What yu going to do with it.'

'I'm going fuck Roy's car, he took Sally to the dance – got in before I could. She's mine not that arse hole's.' He was also thinking about Roy's refusal to sell him some more weed; his own stash had run out a week ago.

'Yeh, that sounds like fun.' Billy yelled, 'Never did like that shit, his dad gives me dad a ha'd time so let's git him.'

Back at the dance, Andrew handed Luke a stick with the fuse inserted. 'Stick it under his car and light it.'

With no one outside the hall Luke crawled up to Roy's car and put the dynamite under the engine. He lit the fuse and ran as fast has he could towards the others. The explosion roared in his ears. The engine crashed its way through the bonnet causing the car to leap up into the air. With oil and fuel trailing after it, the engine arced high in the air followed by other grotesquely distorted parts out of the engine bay. The others took off in the opposite direction. Pieces began to shower down around the running boys. Peter only got a couple of meters before the alternator hit him on the shoulder, he screamed in pain. Luke looked up to see Sally crouching down by his car; she'd come out to find Luke. He took off to protect her, but was knocked off course by a wheel. He regained his feet to see the engine come down on top of Sally.

There she is - a simple grave. The headstone stood up right in the full sunlight, 'Sally Robertson, Born 2nd July, 1997 - cruelly taken - 31st March 2014.' The date burned a hole in his heart, but he continued to look, then it struck him, it didn't say she would be missed, loved or even thought of. But the headstone was wrong, he thought of her every night as he relived the nightmare. He fingered the white collar around his neck and silently prayed that she would forgive him.

Marilyn Linn

Marilyn is a retired school teacher. She enjoys writing short stories and poems, some of which have been successful in competitions and have been published in Australia, New Zealand, Japan and USA. Other interests include reading, craft work, travelling and grandchildren. Marilyn is a member of Seaside Writers' group, Marion Writers' Group and Bindii-the SA Japanese poetry form group.

Apologies to Teddy

A nonsense poem

Edward Lear's appearance was quitaffable
he wore clothes that were oddly winderable
he was known for his absonism
and feared for his obcantism
but his face to the world was reumontable.

Mr Rutherage was fond of thawtering
he flippled the day a-shoedering
he liked to make habbizzle
which induces bright highbozzle
that left Mr Rutherage wrassing.

Young Peter was an exmoniam
who spent time with passing gypsylliam
he danced with the doosic
and kissed all the foosic
young Peter was quite the quontiniam.

Mr Rutherage, Peter and Lear
used words that were often unclear
but we play with the rhyme
and have a good time
all the while turning words on their rear.

Absent Without Permission

Without knocking, Sara threw open the door to her son's bedroom. She took four big steps across the heaps of clothes tossed randomly on the floor, snapped open the blind and thrust open the window.

'Gavin, I'm going to work in a minute and when I get home this afternoon, I expect this room ... this disgusting mess, to be cleaned up. Sort it out! And don't just throw everything in the dirty washing basket.'

Gavin grunted.

'Did you hear me? Either it's done, or you're grounded for the long weekend. And clean the mould off this window ledge. Yuck. The room stinks of rotten sneakers and dirty clothes. It's revolting.'

'Yeah. Okay.'

'I've left you a sandwich in the fridge. Please get this room done, Gavin. Bye.'

Gavin rolled over and wrapped his feather quilt around his shoulders, dragged his pillow over his head, like a cocoon, and went back to sleep.

When he awoke, using as little energy as he could, he

pushed some of the heaps of jumpers, jeans, socks and underwear together. He sat on top of them and sorted the items he could reach into new heaps. Jeans to the right, T-shirts and jumpers to the left and everything else behind him. He threw his sneakers behind the door. Deciding he had accomplished his task, he climbed back into the refuge of his bed.

Sara was home first that evening. She checked the refrigerator and saw the sandwich had gone.

'Are you there, Gavin?' she called in the general direction of her son's room. Silence. She took some meat out of the shopping bag before putting away the rest of the shopping. 'I wonder if Gavin's still in bed. He better not be,' she muttered as she crossed the hall to his door.

For the second time that day, she barged into Gavin's room. From the doorway the room looked much the same as it had that morning. Sara stepped over the heap of clothes nearest the bed and yanked the bedding off revealing the clothes underneath. The bed was empty. She shook the blankets as if to be sure Gavin wasn't stuck in them somehow. She looked around the room and noticed some of the clothes had been moved. 'At least he's made a bit of an effort,' she mused.

Are you in here, Gav? Hello!' She stepped forward and kicked each heap, first gently, then more savagely. Gavin was gone. 'Nuisance,' she said, to her daughter, Lisa, who was watching her mother kick the heaps of clothes. 'Where the hell is he? Do I cook enough dinner for him or not? He's becoming weird, more and more weird. Where is he? Look at all these jars with things growing in them. What are they?'

She closed his window and shut the blind before leaving the room, closing the door behind her. 'He has the light on all night and the blind closed all day. When he gets back, he's definitely grounded.'

As she prepared the evening meal for Rick, her husband, and Lisa, she asked, 'Do you think he'll be home for dinner, Rick? Should I save something for him?' Her voice was sharp with anxiety.

'How the hell would I know? He's turning into a real deadbeat. Can't say anything, except grunt, and I wouldn't be surprised at anything he might have living in his room. No. Don't save him anything. Let him get something himself when he turns up.'

Lisa sat quietly, sensing this was not the time to tell her parents she thought Gavin was moving out. He hadn't told her this, but she had a 'funny feeling'. Her father was right—Gavin was changing. He avoided light in the daytime, he disliked breezes, he slept a lot of the time, seldom washed and was more interested in the things in his jars than in his family or friends. She avoided him at home and at university.

'I haven't seen him around uni this week, but that's nothing new,' she said to no-one in particular.

Gavin didn't come home for dinner that night or the next. Rick went into Gavin's room, made Gavin's bed, and sorted the dirty clothes for Sara to wash.

'I reckon he's got a girlfriend,' decided Rick, as he put away the clean clothes.

'Don't know who she would be; might be a boyfriend,'

offered Lisa, with a shrug. 'Could only be one of his 'lepo' weirdo mates. They're all weird.' Life was peaceful without Gavin around. She secretly hoped he would stay away longer.

By the following weekend, Gavin was still missing, and Sara demanded Rick accompany her to the police station to report their son missing. The police officer was polite but his disinterest was blatantly clear.

'You need to write this information down, don't you?' asked Rick, slamming his hand down on the counter.

Without hesitating or looking at Rick, the police officer suggested Gavin was 'taking time out' and would be home soon. 'He's probably off with a girl somewhere. He'll turn up. Have you contacted any of his friends?'

But none of the family could name any of his friends, girls or boys. He didn't play sport and wasn't into music.

'Calm down. I'll write a Missing Persons Report. Keep in touch with us, and let's know when he turns up.' The officer was dismissive again. No report was taken.

'Thanks for nothing. No help at all.' Rick muttered as he walked away.

Back home, Rick opened Gavin's bedroom door. 'This can stay open while the tenant is AWP—absent without permission—again. He's done this too many times recently. I'm fed up with him. He'd better have a good story when he comes back. He thinks he can use our home as a drop-in centre. He should know we worry about him when he doesn't let us know where he is.'

Rick and Sara did not know what to do next. Their son was missing but the police were not taking it seriously, they thought.

Each time Sara passed Gavin's door, she stopped and looked in.

Another week passed but still no Gavin. Sara and Rick became afraid for the well-being of their son. They went to the police station every day hoping the police might have some good news for them. A Missing Persons' Report was eventually taken.

'We'll let you know if we get any news,' the anxious parents were told. 'We've sent his details state-wide and listed him as a missing person. For now we can do nothing more. Try again to contact his friends. Stay in touch.'

'But his mobile phone is in his room. He never goes anywhere without it. And all his jars of specimens are still in his room . . .' Sara said to the officer at the desk but he just shrugged.

'He's a teenager, a uni student. They do odd things when the hormones kick in. I mean, who studies lepidoptery anyway? What did you say lepidoptery was? About bugs or something, was it? He'll be right,' said the officer, shuffling the report sheets before walking away, carrying his sheets of paper reports, without making eye contact with either Rick or Sara.

'Flicked off, again.' Rick shook his head with despair as he stomped out of the police station. He wanted more than bland words.

Lisa asked around at uni, but no-one had seen Gavin or heard from him. Other students, who Lisa knew only by sight, didn't know where he was. His lecturer said Gavin had zoology assignments due and would fail the semester if they were not in soon.

One night, when it was a little chillier than usual, Sara was walking past Gavin's doorway. She heard a flapping sound and looked in. She saw a huge moth in the room. It was wider than two hands, beating itself against the window. It fluttered towards the bedhead when Sara entered the room.

'Rick. Quick. Come and look at this. What do you think it is?'

Rick heard the panic in her voice. 'Must be one of his specimens, I think.'

Mesmerised, they watched the torment of the moth as it tried to find a place to land, dropping fine dust scales from its wings wherever they made contact with the wall, the window, or the bed. Finally it crashed into Gavin's pillow and stopped, exhausted.

'What are you guys looking at?' asked Lisa as she saw her parents looking into Gavin's room. Sara put out her arm and drew Lisa closer. Lisa's hands flew to her face and she let out a strangled scream, and then burst into hysterical tears.

'What? What's the matter? It's only a wood moth; we've seen them before,' said her father.

Lisa screamed. 'No, Dad. No. It's not a wood moth. Don't you see? It's Gavin.'

Sara fainted.

SPACESHIPS

A thin mattress covered the wooden bench. Toni sat huddled in the corner of the room, her knees drawn up tightly against her chest as she tried to merge with the wall and become invisible. The walls were no particular colour, not blue, not grey, just stark and unfriendly. A stainless steel chamber pot sat beside the bed. A rough grey blanket was folded neatly on the end of the bed.

The screams of the other captives echoed from cell to cell. Screams of pain, anguish, fear – hysterical laughter.

Toni tried in vain to block out the noises and the smells. Smells of unappetising food mixed with the acrid odour of stale urine and pine-fresh cleaning aids. The place was clean, very clean, but an offensive stench hovered over everything.

Doors clanged and reverberated and Toni, a thin middle-aged woman with cropped hair and gaunt eyes, trembled as the sound of clanging doors approached.

Two nurses flung open her door and blocked the exit. Not that she wanted to run. She had decided to co-operate today. Try a different tack.

'Come on, Tiny Toni. Time for your treatment. Hop in the wheelchair like a good girl.'

Fear and nausea swamped her small frame. 'Please don't do this to me,' she whimpered. 'I'm not crazy. Really I'm not. Ask me anything. I'm not a loony. I shouldn't be here. You've made a big mistake.'

'Come on now. Don't make things difficult for yourself. Come and talk to Dr Stan. Tell him about it and maybe you won't have to have the ECT today.'

After her electroconvulsive therapy treatments, Toni's head ached for hours. Some days she could not even talk. She had difficulty answering simple questions or her mother's name or her sibling's names. The same questions, day after day.

'Good morning Toni. How are you feeling today?' asked the short, grey-haired Dr Stan. He had the carbolic look of one who spent too many hours indoors.

Toni's eyes flickered at his high forehead, imagining herself attaching electrodes to him. She didn't answer.

'Are we going to have a little chat today Toni?'

'Why am I here? Why do you keep me locked in like some freak?' Tears gathered on her chin, ready to drop onto her chest if she moved.

'Toni, do you remember what you were doing when we came to rescue you?'

Toni dropped her head and the tears fell, making a wet patch between her meagre breasts. 'I was at the school. I work there. They'll find out I'm here and make you let me go.'

'What were you doing at the school when we came to rescue you Toni? Try to remember.'

'I could remember if you didn't keep torturing me. It makes

my head burn up.' The tears flowed unchecked. Her nose was dripping and, despondently, she wiped it on the sleeve of her hospital gown.

'We have tried to help you Toni. Now we want you to try to remember what you were doing and why. Were you angry about something?'

Toni slumped un-cooperatively in the wheelchair. She gritted her teeth and her eyes flicked from side to side as she struggled to look away from the doctor. The silence was filled with rat-like scurryings outside the closed door.

'Toni let me help you. Do you remember the school?'

She nodded without looking up.

'Good. Can you tell me if it was on a main road or a side road?'

'Main. Busy. Noisy. I remember.'

'Good girl Toni. What else happened there?'

Softly, almost to herself, Toni said, 'They called me names.'

'Who did? The students? The staff?'

'They all did. All those creepy people. I had to cut my hair.'

'Tell me what they said. You are doing very well today Toni. Tell me what they said.'

'"Bony Toni looks like a pony," they said. So I cut my hair off. See – no more pony tail.' She ran her fingers wildly through her cropped hair. 'They said I looked like a witch. So I pretended to cast a spell on them and they all screamed. They're the crazy ones, not me.'

'Good. Good. Now do you remember anything about eggs?'

Toni trembled. Her eyes widened and she stared, unseeing, at the doctor.

'They were chasing me.'

'Who Toni? Who was chasing you?'

'All the coloured spaceships. They were everywhere.'

'Spaceships, you say?'

'I threw grenades at the spaceships to scare them away.' Toni tried to stand up but was unable. She was tied to the wheelchair. 'Let me go,' she screamed, 'They'll come back if I don't stop them.'

'Sit down please Toni. Tell me again about the eggs you were throwing.'

'I don't know what you're talking about. What eggs? Have you been in the sun, doctor? My mother said sun on your head will make you mad. Why can't you understand?' Toni retreated into herself, slumping on the restraints around her.

'Okay Toni. I'm sorry. I interrupted you. You were saying about grenades and spaceships. What were the spaceships doing?'

Toni remained silent in her own world, refusing to look at Dr Stan, or the nurse hovering in the background.

'Tell me about the spaceships. Did they have any lights?'

'There were lots of them. All different colours. All in a line. They came every day. Sometimes one would stop and suck up a student. I hated that. I tried to save those kids, you know, but I never could. Now it's too late.'

'How could you have saved them Toni? Why is it too late?'

'I had to blow them up. I had grenades. I tried to do it. Really I did. I tried to blow them up. I hope they will forgive me.' Toni covered her head with her arms, holding her head down, her chin on her chest, and sobbed.

The doctor and nurse let her cry for a few minutes, then Dr Stan squatted by the side of her wheelchair. 'Toni, today I'm going to give you some medicine. Will you drink it nicely for me, please?'

'Can I go back to my bed then? No ECT? Please?'

'You take this medicine and have a little sleep. Then we'll talk again.'

The nurse handed Dr Stan a medicine glass half filled with whitish-yellow fluid.

'This is called Midazolam, Toni, and it will relax you. If you feel like talking, tell Nurse Jenny. She will let you talk into the tape recorder. We think you'd like that. Now drink up.'

The doctor wrote up his notes as the medication took effect. 'Now off you go and have a sleep. Nurse Jenny will come back later.'

As Toni was being taken to her room, she began to feel light-headed. She swayed from side to side in her wheelchair, giggling to herself. She looked around but her eyes were unfocused, wide open, abnormally bright. 'Nurse, can you loosen this thing round my middle, please? It's hurting me.'

Her voice was steady and clear.

'Sure Toni. Just a little bit.'

'Can I ask one more little favour? Can we go past the big window? I want to see the trees. I love trees.'

'I suppose we can,' replied the nurse. 'How are you feeling? Okay?'

'Nurse, I'm so sorry I have been a bother to you and the nice doctor. Do you know about spaceships? Not everyone can see them, you know. The doctor can't. His mind is closed.'

The nurse paused by the big window which looked out onto a large lawn. 'There you are Toni. It looks lovely out there, doesn't it? Maybe we can go out there for a walk one day. Would you like that?'

Together they gazed past the empty car park to a small group of people walking across the lawn. A small car crawled into the car park. Toni straightened and sat rigidly in the wheelchair.

'Oh no!' she screamed. 'Oh no! NO! They've found me!' she cried. She fought with the sheet which held her in the chair, and threw herself around frantically.

Nurse Jenny grabbed Toni's hands, and held them tightly together in a prayer attitude. 'Stop Toni. You're safe. You're alright. Sit still.' Jenny could see the red panic button just out of reach. 'Toni. What have you seen that has frightened you? Tell me so I can help you. What is it?'

'It's one of them. They're after me. Don't let them see me. Get me out of here.'

Jenny tried to move the wheelchair back, but the brake was on. The emergency button to summon assistance was out-of-reach. To reach it she had to release Toni's hands. She measured the distance with her eyes, let go of Toni and made a dash. In that split second, Toni lurched forward and tipped the wheelchair over, slipping free of the restraints. As Jenny punched the emergency button, Toni launched herself at the window. The shock of hitting the glass stopped her momentarily. With a sudden rush of Herculean strength, Toni turned around, lifted the wheelchair and hurled it at the window.

Emergency lights flashed as the smashing of glass echoed across the neat lawn. A group of walkers stopped in their tracks and gawked at the scene.

Toni leapt through the jagged hole in the glass and rushed at the car that had just parked. The woman driver had hardly put her feet to the ground when Toni grabbed her by the shoulders and flung her down. The woman's head hit the road with a dull thud. She lay quite still.

Toni turned her attention to the car. She picked up a large stone and smashed the front wind screen then violently started pulling at the seat covers, screaming incoherently. Two security nurses grabbed her but she kicked and punched, managing to slip free and sprint off across the lawn. The group of walkers stood aside and watched her flight.

'Grab her. Grab her!' yelled the pursuing nurses.

One of the walkers took a flying dive and brought Toni to the ground with a rugby style tackle, winding her.

Toni stayed just as she had fallen until a medical team came and retrieved her, loading her unceremoniously onto a barouche. She kept saying, 'Now I'll die. They found me. Now I'll die. They found me.'

Toni was taken to the infirmary and restraints secured her to the bed. She lay quietly, staring at the dusty ceiling fan. Dr Stan came and sat beside her. 'What happened Toni? What did you see?'

She turned to him with unseeing eyes filled with tears. 'A spaceship came. Now I'll die. They found me.'

Toni closed her eyes and slipped into a coma.

A few hours later when the nursing staff came to check on her, Toni's bed was empty.

Circles

'Stop. Look over there!' shouted Greta.

'What at?'

'Oh Adam. For a university graduate, you can be so thick. Look at the barley crop. There are three circles in the middle of the paddock half way up the side of that mound. Stop.'

'I can't stop here. Wait a minute,' Adam answered.

Adam pulled the car into a gateway. Greta leapt out. Adam followed and they ran towards the edge of the paddock until Greta stretched her arm out in front of him and they both stopped.

'I think these are crop circles, Greta. I read somewhere they're radioactive. We shouldn't walk over them.'

'I don't think that's true. I suppose you believe in space ships too?'

'Let's have a look at them anyway, now we are here.'

'Whoa! Did you feel the earth move?' Greta turned to Adam, her eyes wide.

'Nah,' he replied.

'There it is again. You must have felt it.'

'I think we should get the hell out of here. Come on.' He

grabbed Greta by her shoulders and pulled her back towards the car.

The ground trembled again.

'I'm scared, Adam.' Greta clung to the front of Adam's tight fitting T-shirt.

He put his arms around her, enjoying the feel of her warm body against his, his mind distracted from the circles.

As the two young people stared at the crop, still clinging to each other, a shiver went through the ground again.

'I think it's just the breeze making the barley move, don't you? I can hear the wind whispering through the seed heads.'

'Let's get out of here.' Adams's voice quavered.

'Are you scared too?' She pulled her head back and looked into Adam's brown eyes and was surprised to see the look of terror.

'Come on. Let's go,' she murmured.

They turned to have one last look, stopped short, and looked again. The centre ring of the circles was moving and it was not the wind. Greta's grip on Adam's shirt tightened and Adam held her closer. As they stood, a strange purple blob advanced towards them, making a slurping noise. Neither of them could move.

The slurping noise grew louder as the blob came closer. Greta screamed and Adam felt her bosom heaving. He tried to run but his legs were paralysed. 'Think South America and the anti-terrorist training we had before we went there. Stay calm. Concentrate on breathing.' he whispered hoarsely into Greta's ear.

'This is not bloody South America,' she hissed.

'Try to kneel down, Grett.'

'I can't.' She was crying now and he felt useless because he could not help her.

The slurping noise grew louder as the purple blob came right up to them, casting a purple haze over everything around them, enveloping them. Everything went black.

Their awareness of time and place was gone when they came to their senses.

'Where are we?' They looked around the large cave-like place they were in. Everything had the same purplish hue they had seen earlier. 'Don't let go of my hand. Try to stay calm. I think we've been abducted.' Adam patted his loose-fitting track pants pockets searching his mobile phone.

'Damn! I've lost it.'

A metallic voice came from behind them. 'Your phone will not work here, Adam. Sit still and be quiet. You will be safe if you obey our instructions.'

Several minutes passed before an odd jelly-looking creature approached through the purple mist. 'We are here on a research project. We will dismantle your vehicle and you will be subjected to some personal tests. We will not hurt you. When we have completed our research, you will be released.'

'My head is spinning. I can't think. I feel like I'm going to vomit. Oh Adam. Where are we?'

'Breathe deeply, Greta,' instructed the metallic voice, 'you will feel better soon.'

'How do you know our names?'

'We have been observing you.'

Greta looked around the cave. She could make out smaller caves around the perimeter but the purple mist made it difficult to see things clearly.

'My name is Yal and I am your host while you are with us. Do you require sustenance?'

After a few moments, Adam answered, 'Yes. That would be good. We'd both like a Subway sandwich and I'd like a beer. Greta would like a gin and tonic.'

They watched the creature slide away into one of the obscure smaller caves.

'What a stupid thing to say, Adam. As if I'd eat anything that thing brings.'

Adam turned his attention to some strange optical effects being displayed on a screen above the exit door where Yal had gone. 'Look Greta, they have some kind of computer in here, but I can't work out the code. I can't work it out at all.'

'Keep working on it. Something might inspire you to try to get us out of here.' Her tone was icy. Adam glanced at her, but she ignored him.

Yal returned with what looked like two ham sandwiches and two cans of cola. Greta refused to touch hers but Adam grabbed his and ate hungrily, remembering he had not had lunch.

'Grett, you need to eat the food and have a drink. You don't know how long it will be before you get anymore.'

'Don't tell me what to do, thank you very much.'

Yal moved through the cave and Greta seized the opportunity to speak. 'Yal, where are you from and why have you captured us?'

'My community lives under these barley fields. The circles are made by our transport. We are on an education journey and want to learn about your modes of transport and your method of collecting solar energy for your vehicle,' he told her in a monotonous metallic tone.

'How long will you be keeping us here? My family will be worried about us.'

'If all goes well, you will be released tomorrow morning. If not, there is no time limit.'

Adam tried to stand up, but an unseen force gently pushed him back down into his strangely curved seat which was similar to a jelly-soft beanbag.

'I'm looking for the toilet,' he said to no-one. He heard a hiss to the left and a small opening appeared. 'I think that might be the toilet,' he told Greta.

'Don't go into something if you don't know where it leads to.'

'Nah. We'll be right. Trust me.'

'Trust you? Why would I trust you? What's your big plan to get us out of here? Have you worked out the computer thing yet? You're supposed to be clever.'

Adam ignored her remarks and found the toilet. On his return he coaxed Greta to stand up and go through the opening before it vanished.

'I don't want to talk to you,' she said as she stood up, legs shaking, and made her way to the toilet.

As she sat down again, Yal returned and announced they were free to walk around but must not touch anything. 'Your touch might cause our computers to malfunction. Keep away from the walls.'

'Before you go Yal, can you tell me what things you are studying here in this field? You said before it was the car you were studying, but there must be more than that.'

'Greta, our people travel all over the Universe to study life on this planet and others. Much of our information is rapidly becoming redundant and we need to refresh our knowledge.' He moved silently away.

'That was intelligent, Greta, now what? Don't forget it was your idea to stop the car.'

'Shut up, Adam.'

Adam sat down. There was very little space to walk around in the claustrophobic atmosphere of the cave. He kept looking with increasing agitation at the computer screen he could see, but was unable to decode any of the digital images.

Greta walked back and forth, peering closely at the walls. Everything was uniformly smooth and mauve and had a slightly metallic odour. She went and stood near the computer screen and watched the icons flashing. She thought she could see through a small section of wall near the screen. Bending forward, her forehead touched the wall. A metallic voice spoke to her. 'Move back. You must not touch anything.'

She was startled and tears sprang to her eyes. 'I'm sorry. I won't touch anything. I didn't mean to touch anything. I'm sorry.'

Yal appeared from a small alcove. 'Greta, we know you did not do that purposefully. Perhaps you need to rest now. Perhaps you need to sleep. Both of you. And Greta, neither of you will remember anything about this when you are returned to your own environment.' It was an order, not a suggestion, spoken with the familiar metallic voice.

'I'm not tired,' said Adam.

'Yes, you are.' the voice said. Yal vanished into one of the indents in the wall.

'Just sit quietly, please Adam.'

Greta looked around the cave, trying to memorise every detail, noting the indents. She had no plans to keep quiet about any of this. She had a list running through her head. 'Walls about two metres high, six sides like a squashed cube, soft looking, mauve and purple everywhere, smell of metal which does not match the soft look of everything, even the inhabitants...' She kept forgetting the details and had to begin again. Adam went to sleep.

Time had no meaning in the cave. Greta tried again to remember details, saying aloud the words, but to no avail.

Eventually, Yal came and announced there were a few tests to be carried out on both Greta and Adam. When Adam was woken from his sleep and he tried to push the purple creature away but, although it looked soft, it was stronger than Adam, Greta observed. When it was Greta's turn, she succumbed and allowed herself to be carried. She was taken through one of the indents to another area and placed on a flat bed, similar to chiropractors' tables, Greta thought.

'We require a blood sample from you, Greta, and one from Adam.'

She began to tremble. She was unable to see Adam and a wash of fear overwhelmed her. A voice in her head kept saying, 'Keep calm. Breathe deeply. Calm, Greta. Calm.'

'No way are you getting any of my blood.' She heard Adam's defiant exclamation nearby.

'You have no choice.' Another creature entered the small cave and held Adam's legs. Blood was drawn from his ankle.

Adam continued protesting. 'Let go of my legs. Get off me.'

'Greta, this will not cause you any pain. We will take a blood sample from your ankle, the same as we have with Adam.

'Why do you need blood?'

'We already have a urine sample and we need a blood sample for our database. If we encounter you again, we will have a match and be able to use the information for our research.' Greta tried to kick and scream. Her resolve to maintain calmness evaporated. Hot tears rolled uncontrollably down her cheeks. Thoughts roared in a tangled cascade through her head. What was happening to them? Would they be released unharmed? Where were they? Why haven't they been discovered and saved by someone? She had no idea who would save them.

After a short interval, Yal came and lifted her. Her arms and legs flopped like a rag doll, her head rested on Yal's soft body. He returned her to the main cave. She could not see Adam and panic set in again. She was aware of her blood racing through her ears and she was shaking. Yal quietly placed a soft, fine blanket over her. 'You will be released in the morning,' he told her.

Adam was returned soon after and he sat in his chair with nothing to say. His stillness disturbed Greta.

'What happened to you?' Greta asked quietly.

'What happened to you?' Adam replied. 'Touch your hair, Grett.'

Greta raised her hand to her head. To her horror, she could feel she had very short hair where her lustrous curls had previously grown.

She screamed out, 'Why did you do that? You cut my hair. I didn't touch anything.'

A voice interrupted their discussion. 'For your information, we also have photographs of your tattoos, Greta, and we thank you for your co-operation.'

'You have tattoos, Greta? I didn't know about that.' Adam raised his eyebrows as he looked at her.

A loud hissing and clunking sound drew their ragged attention and a thick, deep purple fog covered them. They were aware of a deep rumbling and shaking inside the cave. An icy point of concern traced down the line of Greta's spine.

Later, Greta and Adam agreed they must have lost consciousness. When they regained their senses they were on the ground under a tree, beside Adam's disassembled car, near the crop circles. Clouds hung bruised and inert over the barley crops. Greta had difficulty focusing on her surroundings. Everything was a blur. The silence was broken by the cry of a magpie.

The car was laid out in pieces beside them. Tools were arranged with surgical precision for them to use. Greta was still holding the light blanket that had been placed over her inside the cave. Even though the day was sunny and warm, she felt more secure hugging the thin blanket.

With little effort they were able to reassemble the car. They worked with little conversation between them. They had acquired new skills without trying.

With the car reassembled, they abandoned most of the tools provided and continued on their way home. They pulled up in front of the local police station to report their drama.

'Where do you think you've been?' asked the officer, scratching his head, clearly not believing their disjointed story. 'Under the ground, you say? But you don't know where? You're not making any sense. You both look all right, except for the girl's haircut. Who cut it?' He grinned at them. Greta noticed Adam clench his fists so she held his arm. 'My suggestion is to stay off the booze, or whatever, in future.'

'No. You don't understand...' Greta began.

Now it was Adam's turn to restrain her. He took her by the arm and pulled her outside.

As time passed, they could talk to each other about some details of their incarceration but the details were vague. They were never able to tell anyone else about their experience; they had no details at all. Eventually they stopped trying.

Soon after the encounter, a fire burned the paddock they were struggling to tell people about. No-one knew anything about crop circles, only about the fire.

Jennifer Mackenzie

Jennifer writes historical fiction with flawless ease. She has a wonderful grasp of drama and pace. She is currently working on her first novel, which will surprise and entertain. Jennifer's stories have texture, depth and warmth for the human spirit. She cleverly pares back frailty and motivation, a natural raconteur.

The Ancestors

They set out as the weak autumn sun nudged the sky behind them, turning the dull gray of night into a soft pink dawn. Ahead, Fiona could almost pick out the tops of the Paps of Jura emerging out of the mist like three old wise women. Jura, her ancestral home.

The small wooden boat, built for stability not speed, carried six of them in all: Fiona, four German tourists and Young Jock, the skipper. She'd known Young Jock all her life and he'd seemed old even when she was a small child.

'Why is he called Young Jock when he is so old?' she'd once asked Gran.

'Because his father was Old Jock,' Gran had replied, as if that was all that needed to be said. Now here he stood, at the helm of the boat he'd guided across these straits a thousand times. Young Jock, as ancient as the highlands.

'The Corry's quiet today. We'll give her a wide berth anyway,' he said to nobody in particular as he steered south west. Fiona had heard stories about the Corryvreckan ever since she was a child. Stories of fisherman disappearing never to be seen again, of women losing their minds after hearing the cries of the whirlpool in the dead of the night, of the island's children dreaming of lost treasures, buried at sea, deep inside the Corry. But the story that had enchanted Fiona the most was of the young couple, on their way home to Jura from their honeymoon. As they drew near to the area where the whirlpool churned they were surrounded by a curtain of golden light. As they clung to each other they saw in the strange screen the face of a child the child they did not yet know they had conceived.

As a little girl Fiona sat wide eyed listening to these stories but as she grew older she knew them for what they were.

'Fairy tales, Grannie, that's all. It's just a whirlpool. A geological phenomenon located half way between the mainland and Jura, caused by...' Here she hesitated and looked around the room. What was it she learned in Geography class?

'By differences in magnetic pull,' she finished with feigned confidence, hoping anybody listening knew any different.

Gran laughed. 'Aye, you've been at those books again my clever lass. You'll be smarter than us all one day. Just remember, my darling, not everything can be learned from books. Some things you can only know if you put the books down and look and listen. Really listen.'

Gran had been known in the village for having the sight. People would come to her for advice because she often knew things that couldn't be known. She could tell when there was a change about to happen—not just with the weather but with other more significant things. Once she'd saved a child's life. He'd been separated from his family during a cliff walk. As night descended and storm clouds rolled in from the sea, the searchers came to Gran in desperation. She'd directed them to the ledge where the child had fallen and lay unconscious, covered from view by bracken leaves.

There was a time, when she was little, that Fiona too had thought she may have had the sight. But that was before. Before her father's fatal accident on the oil rig and before Mum's drinking. Before she'd been sent away to school. Before the vicious name calling and the endless late nights studying, trying to prove herself. Before the loneliness that now was always with her.

Fiona had come back to Oban a month ago for Gran's funeral and had stayed on. Her plans to return to Edinburgh and begin University seemed all too hard now. Everything seemed hard.

The trip to Jura had been arranged by her uncle. 'Time you went home to meet the ancestors,' he'd said.

Fiona had laughed, wondering if he'd had a few too many whiskies.

'What do you mean, meet the ancestors. They're all gone. And anyway,' she said, with less certainty, 'Edinburgh's my home now.'

'Aye, well, home is where your heart is, right enough,' he said looking at her intently, as if he could actually see into her heart. 'As for the ancestors, well they might be gone from this world but it's time for you to see where they came from, lass. Your ancestral home from before the clearances.'

Fiona had written an essay on the clearances. Of families driven out and cottages burned to make way for the sheep. Her ancestors had fled from Jura to the mainland and hung on there, eking out an existence as shepherds on the mountains during the winter and fishing during the summer. Others had taken their chances in new continents, far away. Some, too proud or too old to flee, had stayed and starved.

The thrum of the boat seemed to have lulled all the passengers into quiet reflection. Drawing her scarf a little tighter Fiona could see the Paps, veiled by a light misty rain, they rose protectively above the tiny village of whitewashed cottages. The still, crisp morning had given way to a gusty wind. Fiona could no longer tell which direction they were heading. The view of the mainland had disappeared and the previously flat sea had become choppy. Menacing waves pushed into them. The boat lurched and Fiona grabbed onto her seat to steady herself. Above the sounds of the wind and the waves she thought she heard an eerie whirring noise.

Within minutes the waves were twelve feet high and seemed to be driving the boat backwards. Back towards the Corry. Fearful, Fiona turned to Young Jock and then to the other passengers. Instead of seeing fear in their faces, as she had expected, it was as if nothing unusual was happening. She shouted to them but they didn't respond. She tried to get up but a gentle force held her in her seat. The boat was getting closer and closer to the whirlpool.

We're going to die, she thought, but instead of feeling fear a comforting calm came over her. She somehow knew that nothing she could do would change their fate. The boat was moving at a great speed, now carried, it seemed, by one massive wave, a wall of water. She could see the edge of The Corry and the black hole at its centre. She said a prayer, a thing she almost never did, and thought of her Gran.

Will I see her there? she wondered. Where she meant exactly she was not quite sure. She noticed that the other passengers and Young Jock had faded, as if life itself had been washed out of them.

Within minutes they'd reached the whirlpool and she could see the menacing tunnel at the centre. They were being pulled down in a spiralling motion, slowly at first then faster. The whirring noise became deafening. The boat tilted until it was almost vertical, yet they all remained seated and breathing, as if gravity and respiration had conspired with the whirlpool to keep them alive.

As they approached the bottom of the tunnel their descent slowed, the boat righted itself and they came to a rest on the ocean bed. Fiona's fellow travellers remained seated but they were now totally translucent. As Fiona stood, the loud whirring noise dropped to a quiet hum. A wall of water surrounded her and in it she saw the faces of her ancestors, as if they had been taken from the family photo album and hung in this watery gallery. They moved towards her and as they encircled her she could hear their gentle chanting.

'You will always be welcome with family. Believe in yourself. Remember your heritage. Look for the good in people. Know you are loved. Use your talents.'

These were the life messages she'd grown up with, handed down from one generation to the next. Messages that she'd put aside since the accident on the oil rig.

She gasped as the image of Gran came forward and placed in her hand a single white shell then withdrew to join the others.

Fiona tried to talk but no sound came. She turned the shell over. It was like the ones she'd collected with Gran as a child. Gran had taught her how to hold it to her ear and hear the sea.

'But how did the sea get in there Gran?' she'd asked back then.

'You put it there,' Gran had replied. 'You and your imagination. See what you can do, Fiona, if you just believe.'

Looking up from the shell Fiona was astounded to see the boat and its passengers safely back on the surface. The Corryveckan was behind them, the whirring had stopped and the ancestors were nowhere to be seen. All she could hear was the throb of the motor and the excited chatter of her fellow passengers. Young Jock stood at the helm guiding the boat into the quay. He turned and winked.

The sea was now mirror flat, the morning mist had disappeared and the green and heather-purple Paps rose in full splendour to greet her. She opened her hands. No shell. She looked behind. No whirlpool. Her relief was quickly followed by sadness. The ancestors were gone. Gran had left her, again.

As she made her way off the quay towards the village she laughed at herself and her foolish daydream. Her cousin Hamish greeted her. She'd seen him at Gran's funeral but before that, not for years. They'd been thought of as twins when they were little, having been born on the same day and having the same broad features, freckles and unruly hair. She looked into his adult face and could still see a resemblance.

'Welcome Fi. You're here safe and sound then? The Corry didn't get you?' he said, laughing. Fiona looked at him. Could he know? His expression gave nothing away.

'Come on. We'll away to my Mum's for a piece and a brew,' he said taking her bag.

As they climbed the hill she noticed a cottage set back from the road. Like most of the cottages on the island it was white, with tiny widows, and walls two feet thick to keep out the icy winter chill. As they got nearer the whirring noise began again, soft and distant, but the same sound as in her dream. The words came to her again, as if Gran were whispering in her ear. 'Look and listen. Really listen.'

'This cottage,' she asked Hamish 'who...?'

As if he knew what she was asking, Hamish interrupted. 'It's where our Gran lived until she married. It's a holiday home now,' he explained, 'empty for half the year. Mum looks after it while the owners are away.'

'Could I have a look inside sometime?' she asked.

'Aye, you can have a keek now.'

As she pushed the door the whirring noise got louder.

'The bedroom upstairs is where Gran was born,' said Hamish.

Fiona climbed the stairs and tentatively pushed the door open. The smell of lavender filled the air. Gran had always smelt of lavender. Fiona went to the window and pulled back the curtains. The view was to the north, towards the Paps. From this direction they lined up, shoulder to shoulder, reminding her of her Uncles as they carried Gran's coffin. Strong, reliable and comforting. A shiver went through her. As she pulled the curtains shut something caught her eye. On the window ledge was a solitary shell. Gran's shell. Her shell.

She picked it up and put it to her ear. The whirring noise stopped and she could hear the sea, just as she had as a child. And was that the sound of chanting too? A simple joy she had not felt for many years enveloped her. The anger, the loneliness and the confusion that had haunted her since her father's death were swept away, at least for now.

Putting the shell in her pocket she went back downstairs. She linked arms with Hamish just as she had as a child and together they stepped outside and made their way up the hill.

Now she knew what it meant to meet the ancestors.

Haydn Radford

Haydn successfully completed his Arts Degree at Flinders University of SA, majoring in Screen Studies, Creative Writing and English. He has a passion for reading short stories and novels, enjoys movies, theatre and live music. Haydn wrote online pieces for Weekend Notes for over 3 years. He had over 230 articles published on a wide variety of topics involving performing arts, music, movies, theatre, entertainment & literary events. He enjoys researching topics, meeting and interviewing people from various walks of life and helps promote and support various causes. As a member of Marion Writers he has written several short stories.

Karma

What perfect weather for a ghost story. The hail lashed at the old slate roof of the bungalow and thunder reverberated overhead. Terry shivered. A tremendous flash of lightning lit up the peninsula revealing the waves crashing over the breakwater. Rubbing his arms to keep warm he thought about what he was going to tell Julie.

I wonder what Julie's thinking, about the other night. We are both adults. It was just one of those things. Anyway, she's so dam sexy, who could blame me? What guy wouldn't be tempted? But I can't let it happen again. If Maud found out, there would be hell to pay. Anyway, I can't dwell on that now. I must remain calm ... Relax ... R-e-l-a-x. I must focus on what I am going to say to Julie.

Another clap of thunder followed by lightning revealed the flailing pines along the foreshore of the marina. He cursed the constant banging of a loose sheet of iron over the veranda. Another job Maud will be expecting me to fix, no doubt, he thought. And it's not even my house. Terry stoked the logs into a raging fire creating flickering shadows around the dimly lit room. He opened a bottle of merlot and took a sip. Nice.

'Hello! You there Terry?' Julie approached along the passageway. She entered the room. Removing her wet coat she hung it over a chair, and stepped closer to Terry by the fireplace. Rubbing her hands together she welcomed the warmth of the fire. 'Step aside or lose a limb,' she said wriggling, showing off her curvaceous body. Her buttoned tight blouse emphasised her breasts and hips. Mindful of Terry looking at her, she tilted her head back slowly, ran her hand through her hair, which lifted her bosom higher.

Stray water droplets glistened on her neck and cleavage. Terry tried not to gape as he handed her a glass of wine. Looking at each other they raised their glasses. She tasted the merlot. 'This is amazing.' Her pink tongue slipped impolitely out to claim some wine at the corner of her mouth. 'Well, you certainly sounded very mysterious on the phone this morning,' she said, moving closer to him. 'Terry, you're beginning to worry me. What is going on?'

He glanced away. His mind was racing.

'I wish you'd just tell me.'

'Julie we need to talk.' He paused. 'I know you'll think I should've said something before, but Maud and Bob were needing another boarder and you were looking for a place.'

She studied him closely. Her tone displayed her growing discomfort. 'If they want more rent? Forget it. I can't afford it.'

'It's not that. And they do like you.'

'Well what's the problem?' She shrugged, looking more confused. 'Does it have anything to do with us...and the other night?'

'No, no.' He looked up over his glass of wine.

'Then, what is it?'

'Julie, There's something I need to tell you about this house.' He paused hunting for the right words. 'It may sound really weird.' Moving towards the Chesterfield lounge, she followed. They sat together.

She considered his demeanour, deciding to hear him out.

'This house was originally the family home of an old man and his two sisters. They were known for their wild parties.'

'And what's wrong with wild parties?' smiled Julie.

Making an effort to sound even more serious, Terry continued. 'It seems they were into the occult. This didn't bother anyone until the disappearance of some young men and women.'

Julie stopped smiling. 'Are you referring to the recent media reports about the discovery of another dismembered skeleton?'

'Yes.' He could see she was hooked. Taking a moment, he placed his glass on a side table. 'It is difficult to imagine now, but years ago, this area was considered remote, with only tin shacks and shanties among the sand hills. It was also a popular rendezvous for young lovers.' With his increasing confidence he continued. 'This house was the first built in the area. Years later the luxury apartment blocks and holiday flats you see along the esplanade followed. People became suspicious of some strange things happening at this house.'

'What's this all got to do with me?' she asked.

'I'm coming to that. It seems the old man began to behave in strange ways towards his sisters. He insisted they get out of his house. They refused, insisting it was their home too. Finally they had a fight and his sisters, being younger and stronger, overpowered him and locked him in his room.'

'Are you telling me that they kept him prisoner in his own house?'

He nodded. 'It gets even better. 'They caught him trying to get out of the house, and in a struggle he had a stroke.' Julie's eyes fixed on Terry. 'They refused to get a doctor, keeping him prisoner in his room. He survived, but they would hear him shuffling around, dragging his left foot.'

Terry paused. He reached to sip his wine.

Julie shivered. 'What happened to him?'

'He died. His sisters didn't report his death. They told everyone he'd moved interstate. But, they buried him under the house.'

'No way.'

'It's true.'

Julie struggled to hold her composure. 'So, what's this all got to do with me.'

'I thought it only fair to tell you. Just in case you heard any strange noises during the night.'

'Any strange noises during the night. Are you kidding? This place creaks and groans all the time.'

'This will sound really weird, but I've actually seen doors open and close slowly for no reason, and strange sounds like something dragging across the floor. I'm surprised you haven't heard anything. It happened again only last week.'

'If this is some kind of joke, Terry, it's not funny. You're really beginning to frighten me.' She drained her glass and put it down on the side table. 'Some evening this turned out to be.' She looked into the fire watching the flames. Terry studied her closely, telling himself, the first one who speaks loses.

'If you're trying to frighten me you're doing a good job of it.' Julie tried to gather her thoughts, looked past Terry at the shadows flickering across the room. 'Why wasn't I told about this... this haunted house and this ghost, or whatever it is, before I moved in? I thought you were my friend.'

'Not everyone is bothered by the sounds. Besides, Maud and Bob need boarders to help pay their mortgage and upkeep of the house.'

As if on cue, bang...bang the sheet of iron flapped up and down.

'Upkeep of the house?' She scowled, gesturing towards the veranda. 'You've got to be joking! It's a right disaster area. The bathroom drainage is a health hazard.' Her tone increasing. 'What was once a big, beautiful house is now old, and run-down. I only took the room because it's so cheap.' Her eyes narrowing, 'You knew I needed cheap digs to complete Uni.' She pointed like she was taking aim. 'You actually described it as a fun place with great parties. You even talked about having a twilight party with everyone getting dressed up as vampires, witches, and zombies. But now, after what you have told me, I'm out of here.'

'Nothing has changed. We could still have some great parties.'

'Over my ...' Her blue eyes continued to hold his.

'I thought someone might say something to you. I felt I should at least warn you.'

'Gee, thanks Terry, you're a real pal.'

'You know, just in case some night you might hear something.'

'Oh. Really?' She stood up. 'Terry, screw you and screw your haunted house.'

***

'So tell me Terry, how's it going with you and Julie?' asked Maud, as they cuddled together.

'Okay, I suppose.'

'You wouldn't know anything about a bloody ghost that makes dragging noises by any chance?'

'Maud, I did it for us.'

'Congratulations Terry. Julie's moved out on account of you and your bloody ghost story. The mortgage is due next week. I was counting on her rent.'

'We'll get another uni student, Maud. I told you, I thought Julie saw me leaving your room the other morning. She hasn't said anything. But what if she did say something to Bob when he returns from Roxby?'

'About these ghost stories of yours, you want to be careful what you wish for.' She propped herself up on one elbow studying him closely. 'Have you heard of karma?' She paused, continuing to give him a feeling of discomfort. 'I understand how you didn't want Julie to say something to Bob, but did you really have to scare her so much with your horrific story.'

'I did it for us.'

'So you keep saying.' Positioning herself, face-to-face, 'Terry, if I found out you were foolin' around with someone else, I'd be your worst nightmare come true.'

'Maud you're talking crazy,' he tried to coax her closer. She showed no interest. 'Maud, you know I love you, and only want you.' He kissed her lightly on the neck. She remained still. His kisses extended up around her ear.

Gently poking him she emphasised every word, 'Just-make-sure-you-do.' Then with a flirtatious look she placed her hand around his neck and gently pulled him closer looking directly into his eyes and kissed him on his lips. He returned her kiss, but felt more at ease with his eyes closed.

Terry tossed and turned. Maud slept soundly beside him. He cursed and looked again at the clock; 3:14am. His latest ghost story just wasn't coming together. Too many loose ends. He felt so tired, just thinking about it. He tried to relax, closing his eyes again. He drifted into a restless dream.

He heard the floorboards creak in the passageway. There it was again. A dragging sound followed by a distinct thump, approaching slowly, stopping at the bedroom door. The door squeaked open.

Terry turned to Maud, still sleeping peacefully. The dragging sound entered the bedroom. He strained to see. There was no-one there. The sound moved closer and he felt an icy grip take hold of his arms. He struggled to wriggle free, but couldn't. His chest pounded, his lips parted. He couldn't raise a sound.

He felt himself being raised and carried shoulder height out of the room, and along the candle lit passageway. *Where am I?* he wondered. We don't have any candles. Passing a mirror he saw his reflection. There was nothing holding him. Fear took hold. A sense of panic permeated him. In a vacant room an old man stood with a shovel and a flickering lantern, beside a gaping, dirty hole. 'Welcome,' he said with a raucous laugh. 'I've been so looking forward to this moment.'

'I've just the place for you,' said the old man. He pushed Terry towards the hole. Terry resisted, but the old man was too strong. Slipping in the loose dirt Terry fell backwards into a hole, landing with a thud. He looked around and then up. It must have been 3 metres deep.

He heard the old man laughing as he shovelled the cold damp earth upon him. 'What a great ending to your story...'

Terry was still unable to make a sound. He got to his feet and tried to climb out, digging his fingers into the clay, but he only slid back down. The dirt showered on him, getting into his nose and mouth.

He gasped for air. His chest wracked with increased pain. His body went into spasm of pain as he sank slowly into a deep sleep.

Morning sun streaked into Maud's bedroom. She woke with a start, eyes focused on the flashing figures – 4.15AM.

'Oh no, not again,' she cried, 'another power failure.' Outside on the driveway she heard voices. She listened closely. 'Oh shit, it's Bob. He's home early,' she cried. She turned over to Terry.

Pulling on his arm, 'Terry wake up! Terry please, Wake up!' Shaking him she pleaded, 'Terry you've got to get up.' He didn't respond. She grasped his cold stiff hand.

Beverley Rainsford

Beverley has had a lifelong interest in mythology, has been a member of several writing groups and is currently writing a fantasy trilogy involving fairies, elves, gnomes and a dwarf. She has spent many holidays on and around the Murray River and visits Melbourne Zoo with her granddaughter regularly.

In My Mind

You have to be the bossiest Guardian Angel in existence. My very own personal demon, according to Daddy. You even insist on choosing my toys. How often must I tell you, I prefer farm sets with stables and horses or inflatables for the pool. It's you who likes Barbie dolls and puzzles. At school you nag me to sit next to Lily Rose when you know Becky is my best friend. You bullied me into wearing Aunty Michelle's old, faded, blue velvet dress with the tear in the hem, to Emily's party. You said the lace collar was stylish. Nobody wears lace collars.

'Did your invisible angel choose it?' everyone teased, putting their fingers behind their ears and wriggling them.

Do you remember when Grandma took Becky and me to the zoo? The instant we walked through the gate you whinged for an ice cream. I tried ignoring you but you wore me down.

'It's for my guardian angel,' I pleaded.

'Tell her she has to wait until after you've had your lunch.' Grandma was firm. She is the only adult who believes you exist. Which for some reason infuriates you.

'Can we have lunch early?' I asked. I find waiting in long queues watching my favourite foods sell out, a real bore.

'An excellent idea,' Grandma replied. 'We'll eat on the lawn next to the playground.'

Becky and I decided on wedges with sour cream. You wanted a hot dog with sauce. What difference does it make when I'm the person who actually eats it? We walked from stall to stall searching for a hotdog. All we found was a sausage sizzle. The smell of smoke and meat made my tummy rumble.

'Will this do?' I asked aloud.

'I hate sausages,' you screamed, inside my head.

'My guardian angel hates sausages,' I repeated, for Grandma and Becky's benefit.

'Then she will have to go hungry.' Grandma waved to the turnoff up ahead. 'Since we've walked this far, we'll visit the tigers.'

'Tigers,' you grumbled. 'I hate tigers. I'd rather see the meerkats.'

Grandma refused to be swayed.

'This way,' she insisted, taking hold of Becky's and my hand, leading us down a path bordered with bamboo and fake rocks. The viewing window was crowded with families with prams and crying babies. A mum was yelling at her kids and a man was posing people for a photo. 'There's another window opposite.' Grandma ushered us on.

'This is boring. I want to see the meerkats,' you groaned.

'Later,' I replied.

'Now!' you shrieked. I could feel your anger burning into my brain.

'Be quiet.' I slapped my hands over my ears, which is dumb

since you're inside my head.

'Hey look, a little birdie.' You had gone from cranky to cheerful in seconds. Or so I believed as I glanced around the enclosure.

A bird was flying towards a tiger dozing in the grass. I held my breath as it flitted above the tiger's mouth, glided between its ears and down its back. Quick as a flash the tiger leapt to its feet and twisted round to chase the bird. To my amazement the bird flew straight at us. The tiger kept right behind it and was gaining speed. They were both getting closer. The bird should have flown into the sky.

'Make it fly higher,' I begged you. I felt desperate; the tiger looked ready to pounce. I grabbed Grandma's hand.

'It's okay,' she said, squeezing my fingers when the tiger slammed into the viewing screen. The bang was so loud I thought the screen had shattered. I'm sure it vibrated. Paws, teeth tongue and throat blurred into blackness. I was certain we were going to be torn to pieces. The tiger fell backwards its yellow eyes glaring hatred at us, at me in particular. I think its mouth was still open. I remember its teeth looked stained. It was terrifying. My whole body was shaking. Its nostrils quivered, its ears twitched and its tail swished back and forth in the dirt.

'I want to go,' screamed Becky.

'Poor Becky,' you giggled, meanly. Truth is, you have a strange effect on animals. Lily Rose's pet budgie shivers and refuses to leave its cage, dogs are wary of you, cats seem oddly curious. Did you slip inside the poor bird's head? Torment it into risking its life, to scare us? Did you?

Because of the excitement the people at the other viewing window rushed over to where we were. By the time they arrived the tiger had stalked off. I could tell it was angry because it kept staring over its shoulder at us as it waded into a creek at the back of the enclosure. It was still staring as it crouched in the water. I had the feeling it was beaming threats at us. Becky reckoned it was embarrassed.

'Nonsense,' said Grandma. 'Who wants an ice-cream?'

Grandma said we should visit the meerkats next, despite them being on the opposite side of the zoo. The viewing screen was packed with children and adults.

'There has to be a reason,' said Becky.

'Babies,' you hissed.

'Babies,' I blurted.

'Oh, I love babies.' Becky tried wriggling between two adults wearing backpacks. It was impossible; she ended up getting biffed on the chin.

After a long wait during which you complained non-stop we managed to push our way to the front. The meerkats were standing on their hind legs in a circle.

'Hiding their babies,' said the girl, next to us. Each time a baby pushed through their legs, several of the adults would scurry after it, leaving a gap for the other babies to escape. They darted off in every direction, some of them coming up to the viewing screen. Their faces were tiny with weeny whiskers and twitching nostrils. It was cute and exciting, especially when the remaining adults chased after them, trying to herd them into a new circle. Even you laughed. As soon as the babies were back in place behind the adult meerkats the boys in the crowd would bang on the glass in an attempt to start them off again, despite their parents watching. You told me to toss grass over the viewing screen.

'Wimp,' you taunted, when I refused. Two of the fathers climbed onto the rock wall at the side of the enclosure to take photos. There is a sign prohibiting it. People often behave badly in your presence.

The tortoise enclosure is across from the meerkats. A girl in denim overalls had climbed over the fence and was hitting a big, old tortoise on the head. It just sat there, letting her. Her back was to us making it impossible to see her face. When the keeper told her to get back on the other side she ignored him.

'Make her,' I pleaded with you.

'There are limits to my powers,' you replied. As the keeper was taking his phone out of his pocket the girl's mother showed up. She had quite a bit of trouble getting the girl to climb back over the fence. The girl kept hitting the tortoise.

'She's autistic,' Grandma whispered, ushering Becky and I back to the meerkats. Your casualness made me more angry with you than usual. It was a harmless old tortoise for goodness sake.

Grandma likes the butterflies best. Being the school holidays the cage was crowded with mums shrieking at their kids to sit on the railing or smile in front of a flowery bush while they snapped photos. The kids were noisier than their mums. Grandma suggested we sit on a wooden bench in the corner.

'If we keep still and have nice thoughts,' she smiled. 'A butterfly might land on us.'

'They seem jittery.' Becky pointed to the ceiling where most of them were circling. We sat for ages. I fidgeted with Becky's bangle, knowing the butterflies were avoiding us because of your foul mood.

'I'm thirsty,' you kept muttering. 'It's hot in here.'

'Then wait outside,' I growled. Since when did you feel heat?

If a butterfly did flutter near Grandma or Becky some kid or their parent would race across to snatch at it. Especially if it had blue wings. When a butterfly landed on Grandma's glasses a girl raced over and grabbed at it. Granny glared at her and told her to stop before she crushed its wings. Grandma could be strict if she had to. The girl's mum said the butterflies were for everyone to enjoy.

'Squashing helpless insects is cruel,' Grandma replied. Grandma and the mum had a long staring competition. Grandma won. We saw them again near the exit. The girl had climbed over the railing and was picking the flowers. Did you put the idea into her head?

Because of your bad behaviour at the zoo Mummy took me to a child psychologist. She had red hair, thick make-up and large, splotchy freckles on her arms.

'There's a toy box in the corner,' she gushed. Her smile was scary fake, especially with the scarlet lipstick. I studied the wall, decorated with rabbits dressed in pink blouses or blue shirts and trousers. 'You play while Mummy and I have a chat.' Play? How old did she think I was?

'Off you go.' Mummy gave me a push. I knew she was nervous, she kept rubbing her nose, so I walked over to the box.

There was a giraffe with a bent neck, a teddy wearing a white tutu, a plane with a broken wing and wooden blocks. A stack of paper and some crayons lay on the floor. I pretended to draw while I listened. Mummy was telling the child psychologist I could understand everything she said.

'It's impossible.' The child psychologist sounded convinced. 'The brain cells of a nine year old are still developing.' Mummy argued but the child psychologist had a louder voice. After a while Mummy gave in.

'She has an invisible friend,' she whispered. 'Who she calls her Guardian Angel.'

'Invisible companions are common in both normal and emotionally disturbed children,' replied the child psychologist. Emotionally disturbed! I could feel my face flushing. Emotionally disturbed. It would be interesting to see how she would cope with someone mean living in her head, giving her nightmares. Huge, hairy apes swinging through the jungle, grunting and squealing. The beady, brown eyed one with saggy breasts, peering down at me, picking at my fur. Yes, I have orange fur.

'Say hello to Mum,' you always taunt. Then there is the dark skinned man with oriental eyes and drooping moustache, chasing me through cobbled alleyways slashing a curved sword. A scimitar, according to you. The baby with the red, wrinkly face makes me want to cry. Sometimes I wake up choking. The black robes, white lilies, the flicker of candles, the reek of smoke, a tiny coffin, sobbing, the hill of soil, the chill beneath me, the chanting.

I was still thinking about my nightmares when the child

psychologist called me over. She sat me in a low chair especially for children while she made a fuss of my drawings.

'What makes you happy?' She looked up, smiling as if she was going to gobble me. Lipstick smeared her two top teeth. I gazed for a long time at the yellow buttons on her green cardigan. Adults are clever at asking trick questions.

'The beach,' I finally answered.

'Why?'

'The water,' I replied. She kept staring at me as if I should say more. 'And the sand,' I muttered.

'Finish this sentence. I feel sad when...'

'My friends tease me.'

'Do they tease you often?' She twisted her mouth into an even scarier smile.

'Depends.' I folded my arms into my tummy and squeezed my legs together. My knees were trembling.

'I feel excited when...'

'Mummy lets me sleep at Becky's.'

'Do you feel safe?'

'I have a Guardian Angel.' I regretted it the moment I said it.

'Is she here now?'

'She's at home.'

'Does she talk to you?'

'Sometimes.'

'Does it upset you when people ask about her?'

'Depends on what they ask.' It was a silly question.

'Does she make you feel safe?'

'She makes me angry.'

'Why?'

'She tries to control my life.'

'Why?'

'Because she has been forgotten.'

'Forgotten. By whom?'

'Mummy, everyone.'

'Why have they forgotten her?'

'She's a stone.'

'Your guardian angel is a stone?' she repeated. I could tell my answer had pleased her because she scribbled in her notebook. 'Does she have wings?'

'She's a stone.' I hate it when grown-ups make fun of me.

'Could you draw a picture of your Guardian Angel for me?' She flared her nostrils. I could hear her breathing.

'She's covered in darkness and sadness,' I whispered.

I knew Mummy was disappointed with the session. I overheard her telling Daddy.

'I told you shrinks are a waste of money,' he grumped. Mummy hates yelling; it gives her a headache. Perhaps I should have pretended you were imaginary, like everyone says. I studied my reflection in my bedroom mirror. Our reflection, you insisted. The concentration sometimes lets me see into your world. My eyes felt dry; I wanted to blink.

'Are you really my Guardian Angel?' I demanded. 'Or a demon stealing my soul?' My breath fogged the surface. I reached across to wipe it clear. Because the humming in my head was making me drowsy I grabbed the corner of my dressing table, knocking the photo of Mummy and Daddy onto the floor. I leaned down to pick it up.

It broke the spell.

'I keep telling you, you have to stay focused,' you snapped.

'I was focused, besides Mummy's angry with me.' I glanced around my room.

'You're small potatoes. She's worried because she's been booked into hospital for a procedure.'

'What kind of procedure?' It sounded scary.

'She's having problems getting pregnant.'

'Mummy wants a baby?'

'Of course she does,' you crowed.

'Why are you excited?' I had a bad feeling. 'Are you planning on getting inside its head.'

'Would you be jealous if I did?'

'You mustn't. It's too cruel.' The thought of you bullying a tiny baby horrified me. Somehow I had to stop you.

'How do you get rid of a guardian angel?' I asked Grandma.

'Ignore her.' She gave me a hug. 'It'll be tough to begin with but eventually she'll get the message.' Tough was right. Becky's parents had invited me to spend a week of the summer holidays with them, on a houseboat. We would be sleeping in bunk beds, swimming in the river, jumping off an old inflated tube from a tractor tyre, exploring backwater islands, fishing, crabbing, staying up late. It was the perfect opportunity to break your hold on me.

'We're finished,' I told you. 'Find someone else to bully.'

'Actually I've decided to stay with Mummy.' You sounded awfully smug. If it was possible I would have thumped you.

'Leave her alone,' I yelled. 'She's my mummy.'

'She's both our mummies.'

'Liar, liar, liar.' My hatred for you flared.

'Have fun on your holiday,' you tittered.

It turned out to be the best holiday I've ever had. Especially as Becky's parents let me steer the houseboat. Her dad even lent me his fishing cap to make it official. I clasped the wheel with both hands, expecting it to be heavy and stiff to turn. It was so easy it rotated half a circle before I realised.

'Oops,' I gulped, worried the houseboat would spin into the shore. When it continued in a straight line I knew it was your doing. You had followed me despite my telling you to stay away. I was really angry, really, really angry. I wanted to show you I was the boss; which is why I spun the wheel in a full circle. The boat slowly veered towards the bank. There were gum trees with low branches hanging in the water.

'You're to going crash.' You giggled, as if it was funny.

'Leave me alone,' I screamed, tugging the wheel backwards. After a nerve-racking wait the houseboat returned to course. I thought I had beaten you, until the boat kept on swerving.

'Here, let me help.' Becky's dad grabbed the wheel. 'Steering a vessel this size is tricky. There's a delayed reaction.' He laughed. Do you know how embarrassed I felt?

After everyone had had their turn at steering, Becky's dad dropped anchor while we had lunch. Watching people eat tends to upset you. Much to my relief, you were silent. It was getting hot and Becky's mum suggested we look for a sandy beach for a swim. There was a rubber dinghy with a petrol motor and oars for emergencies, attached to the stern of the houseboat. Becky and I had been itching for a ride from the moment we discovered it.

'Time for a test drive,' said Becky's dad. We rushed off to change into our bathers leaving him to launch the dinghy. As soon as we climbed in, he started the engine. Becky and I wanted to explore some of the islands in the swampy backwater on the far side. We could hear birds squawking and the shadows from the trees gave it a spooky look.

'It will be humid and smelly,' warned Becky's dad, steering towards the nearest island.

He was right; the place ponged. Tree roots and fallen branches jutted from the bank and there were stagnant pools, covered with larvae. We had to slap madly at the mosquitoes swarming around us.

'Where's the insect repellent?' Becky scratched at the red lumps on her arms and legs.

'Back on the houseboat,' you sniggered.

'These darn mossies will spoil our campfire tonight.' Becky's mum stamped her feet, flapping her thongs. Her big toe had three bites.

'I'll light some citronella candles. If we wear sleeves and long socks we'll be fine,' replied Becky's dad.

'Meanwhile let's have a swim.' Becky's mum turned towards the dinghy.

'Take a last look at your prized swamp,' you said, in your smart-alecky voice. She's too sensible to come back. I stuck my stick into a pile of rotting, black muck and stirred. All sorts of creepy crawlies were hiding in the dampness. I wished I had brought a jar.

'Shut up,' I hissed at you.

There was a sandy stretch of beach much further down the river which Becky's parents reckoned would be perfect for a campfire. I still got bitten on my wrists and thumb. Becky's mum wanted to cook sausages but her dad insisted on the steak.

'First night is special,' he said, splashing the meat with port. Becky's mum wrapped potatoes in foil and wedged them between two logs at the bottom of the fire. She put four bananas on the top log. Becky and I toasted marshmallows while we waited for the food to cook. You teased me because I kept burning mine.

'A spider!' Becky shrieked, dropping her fork into the flame.

Becky's dad had put a fresh log on the fire and a big, hairy spider ran along its length. On reaching the end it dipped a leg over the edge, as if it was testing the heat. The flames burnt the leg off. It was obvious the spider was in a panic because it darted back to the other end and dipped another leg.

The same thing happened. It would have hurt. My face felt hot and tight just from leaning close and my eyes were dry. I realised later I had singed my fringe.

'Your time is over mate.' Becky's dad poked a stick at the spider, making it rear onto its back-legs. It lashed at the stick with its remaining front-legs.

'It's fangs are open ready to bite,' you laughed. I stared at its weeny green eyes, flashing in the fire glow.

'Stop teasing it,' I pleaded. Becky's dad dropped the stick into the fire. The spider continued its running. Every time it got to the end of the log it would dangle another leg. Finally with only two legs left, it plummeted into the coals below. I heard the tiniest hiss.

'It will now have a fear of fire,' you said.

'It's dead,' I whispered.

'Same as me.'

Earlier in the day Becky's dad had tied several yabby cages to dead tree branches jutting from different spots in the river. He wanted to check the cages before bedtime.

'Can we come?' asked Becky.

'Next time,' he replied, revving the dinghy's engine, chugging towards a branch. As he was pulling in the first cage, a huge splash caused the river to heave. Our houseboat creaked, rose and fell on the swell.

'Blimey,' gasped Becky, as we watched the waves lapping onto the shore.

'Souls,' you murmured. 'They sleep through the day and come out at night.'

'I wish you would sleep through the day,' I muttered, toeing the arcs of frothy bubbles.

The river had settled by the time Becky's dad returned.

'Did you see what caused the splash?' Becky asked him.

'Too dark. Probably some old bunyip fishing for his supper.'

'Shush. You'll give her bad dreams. Bunyips are pretend.' Becky's mother was staring at me. I know she thought I was a screw loose. Everyone did.

'Bunyips don't scare me,' I said, walking into the shallows to prove it, knowing you would warn me if there were any about.

Becky's dad had strung the cages to the back of the dinghy.

We all helped drag them onto the sand. They were chock-a-block with yabbies, clinging onto each other and clacking loudly. Becky's dad wedged the barbecue tongs under one, to flip it onto the sand. As it was crawling back to the water he grabbed it by its claws and held it up while her mum shone the torch on it. It was massive, easily four times the size of the brown yabbies in Grandpa's dam. It kept snapping its pincers at us. They were a purply blue colour. Its eyes were like glued on black, plastic beads and it had a white underbelly.

'It's been feasting on dead humans,' you said. I knew you were trying to freak me out.

'What do yabbies eat?' I asked Becky's dad. He rolled his eyes.

'Two campers drowned here, a few weeks ago. According to the locals, by the time the police retrieved their bodies they had been gobbled to the bone.'

'Gossip,' said Becky's mum.

Becky's dad put three of the yabbies into the overnight net with a catfish he had caught earlier in the day. I felt sorry for the catfish. It was greyish and had whiskers. Admittedly the spike on its back looked dangerous.

'See who survives.' Becky's dad crammed the remaining yabbies into an old foam Esky. They kept clambering on top of one another and had to be pushed down with a mallet. Their crunching and chomping noises gave me the shivers.

'They're angry,' you said, as Becky's dad slammed the lid down. The Esky was too heavy to lift and had to be dragged across the gangplank into the houseboat. We were standing in the kitchen area watching the lid jiggle when a claw appeared.

'Darn.' Becky's dad dashed ashore to fetch a large rock. By the time he returned, a yabby had climbed onto the rim and the lid was sliding off. 'Problem solved,' he assured us, knocking the yabby back in, plonking the rock on the lid. 'Who's for bed?'

Next morning I woke early. For some reason I was extra thirsty. Becky was snoring in the bunk above. Slipping my legs from under the blanket I swung them onto the floor.

'Eek!' I screamed, bounding back onto my bed. I had trodden on a yabby.

'What?' Becky's head appeared from the top bunk.

'I ha ha hate you.' I hugged my knees to my chest, rocking back and forth in an attempt to calm myself.

'What have I done?' Becky sounded angry.

'Not you.' I quickly glanced up, horrified at Becky's misunderstanding. 'It's my Guardian Angel.'

'You're blaming me?' you shrieked.

'Who else would let a yabby loose?' I poked my fingers against my forehead, to let Becky know I was talking to you.

'They chomped through the Esky during the night.' You said it sarcastically. 'I warned you they were angry.'

'Liar! Liar, liar!' I screamed, over and over.

'Stop it! Now!' You pressed yourself into my brain, to let me know how angry you were. 'It's always the same with you. Remember the zoo. You blamed me when the tiger crashed into the viewing screen. It was also my fault the butterflies had the jitters and the adults behaved worse than their stupid kids.'

'You kept complaining.'

'Because you were ignoring me. You always do when you're

with your precious Becky.'

'Becky is my friend.'

'And what am I? Your enemy?' You said it, expecting me to disagree.

'Dad reckons you're my personal demon.' I regretted it the moment it slipped out of my mouth.

I would have apologised, only Becky put her arm around my shoulders. She had climbed down to my bunk while we were arguing.

'Is your invisible angel being mean to you?' she asked.

'The yabbies are loose.' I rested my head on her shoulder. 'I trod on one. It could have bitten me.' I kept imagining huge, purple pincers ripping great chunks of flesh off my foot, crunching my bones, blood pouring everywhere.

'Oh.' Becky peered at the floor.

'Tell her!' you yelled. 'Tell her you're blaming me.' I bit my lips, determined to ignore you. But you kept on. 'If you want an update on Mummy, you have to tell her,' you bossed!

'Mummy?' I had been having so much fun I had hardly thought about Mummy. 'Is she okay?'

'She's fine.' It was Becky who answered. She was my friend, my best friend. 'Your invisible friend is teasing you again. You have to block her out. I can hear Mum and Dad talking. I have to warn them the yabbies have escaped before they tread on one.'

'I'll go.' I leant over the side of the bunk, looking for my shoes.

'We'll both go.' Becky took hold of my hand. It was scary and exciting at the same time, creeping down the narrow passageway, expecting to get bitten at any moment. We froze at every creak and rustle.

'What's wrong?' called Becky's mum, when we both screamed at the same time.

There were three big holes in the Esky and it was empty.

'Stay on your bunks.' said Becky's dad. 'While I search the boat.' Yabbies were everywhere, under chairs, my wet towel and shorts, two were behind the toilet. A few sickly ones had wandered outside and had to be tossed overboard.

'The sun's dehydrated them,' said Becky's mum. Becky's dad put the healthier yabbies in the blue, plastic Esky we used for drinks and snacks when we went ashore. Because nobody had bothered to count them we had to keep our shoes on and stay alert for strays. During breakfast Becky and I tucked our feet under our bottoms. I kept imagining I could hear them scuttling about.

After breakfast Becky's dad hauled in the overnight net and emptied it onto the deck. The catfish twisted back and forth, thumping its body and gulping air. Its gills were flapping so hard I could see red veins. The yabbies were strangely still.

'What's wrong with them?' asked Becky. Her dad flipped one onto its back. Its belly was missing. It was amazing, considering the size of their nippers. Did you put them in a trance?

'The spike on the catfish's back is poisonous,' said Becky's dad. 'Giving it the advantage.'

'Oh.' I tried to picture the catfish stabbing the yabbies. It would had to have been freakishly fast and either super bendy or able to swim upside down. Or maybe it was already at the bottom of the net and jabbed their underbellies. Though with three yabbies and one catfish, surely the yabbies would have ganged together to nip out its eyes or bitten a hole in its belly.

Standing close to Becky I watched her dad hold the catfish down while her mum snipped the spike off with wire cutters. The catfish thrashed and wriggled. It made me feel sad, especially when he cut the head off. The bone made a crunchy, grating sound.

'At least its free,' you whispered.

'It's dead,' I said.

'I'm talking about its soul,' you replied. Once the catfish had been skinned Becky's mum placed it in a bowl of salty water to soak. We were going to eat it for dinner, with tomato, cucumber and lettuce salad.

The yabbies were for lunch. Becky's mum boiled water in a casserole pot. Her dad used the barbecue tongs to push them into the steaming bubbles. They went berserk. It was incredible how far they could open their claws and curl their tails.

'Behave you nasty blighters.' Becky's dad had to dip each claw separately. They were very stubborn and cleaved to the tongs refusing to let go even after turning scarlet. Sometimes he had to knock them off with the meat mallet. At first I thought you were urging them on, until I realised they were fighting for their life. Maybe if I was being lowered into boiling water, I would do the same. It was a scary thought.

It took the entire morning to shell the yabbies. There was enough meat to fill four cereal bowls and a plastic container. We ate them with mayonnaise Becky's mum made from egg yolks, oil, tomato sauce and chopped onion. Although it sounds yucky it actually tasted nice. Becky's dad said their meat was white because they lived in sand. And ate dead people, I was tempted to say.

The days went quickly, probably because you had finally left. It was weird being able to have my own opinions without having to worry about hurting your feelings. We fished, caught more yabbies, swam, jumped off the rubber tractor tube and visited several islands in the dinghy. Because they were swampy, buzzing with mosquitoes and smelt of rotten leaves, we wore insect repellent and proper shoes. Becky and I collected creepy crawlies. Sometimes we saw birds or heard rustling and thumping. Once it sounded like a whole tree was falling over.

'Possums,' said Becky's dad.

I got sunburnt lying on my towel, on the roof of the houseboat, wondering where you had disappeared to and who you were bothering. I had a bad feeling it was Mummy. If you dared to annoy Daddy he would put a curse on you. For some reason the yabbies reminded me of you. I kept wondering if they had had past lives. And if they were now in some damp, dark place, chatting to the living yabbies, warning them to scram before they got eaten.

Becky and I were putting fresh soap in the shrimp nets when we heard her mum swearing.

'What's wrong,' we yelled, running into the kitchen area. She was staring at a plate on the sink, heaped with bright, green sausages.

'Blimey,' muttered Becky.

'I'm sorry,' I stammered, blushing with embarrassment. 'My

Guardian Angel must have done it.'

'Nonsense.' Becky's mum hugged me. 'I forgot to remove them from the plastic bag. The butcher warned me they would perspire.'

'They're luminous...like the plastic stars on my bedroom wall.'

'Bacteria. They've gone off.'

We chucked the sausages into the river. They looked like poos, bobbing in the wake of the boat. Rats as big as possums leapt from the overhanging trees. At least I assume they were rats. They made huge splashes. It was the only time we saw them in daylight.

On the last morning of our holiday we had to swab the decks, cram our gear into our suitcases, wash the breakfast dishes and have a shower. The last person often got cold water.

'Let's soap ourselves first and rinse off together,' suggested Becky. We had so much fun sloshing water at each other we forgot to hurry and ended up freezing. The drive home took forever because of all the traffic. I was desperate to see Mummy and slightly curious to see if you were there.

The moment we pulled into my drive I opened the car door and ran towards Mummy, who was standing on the veranda.

'Mummy, Mummy, I missed you,' I yelled, hugging her tightly. 'And you too Daddy.' I swapped over to him.

'Did you have fun?' he asked, swinging me onto his shoulders.

'It was fantastic. You should have seen the yabbies. They were enormous.'

Once we had taken my bags inside and Becky and I had drunk a glass of lemonade we were sent outside to play while the grown-ups had coffee. I wanted to stay and hear about Mummy's procedure at the hospital.

'We can listen through the window,' said Becky. It was difficult because they were whispering. Fortunately Daddy has a loud whisper.

'A calcified foetus,' he said.

'What's a calcified foetus?' asked Becky.

'Shush.' I stretched onto my tippy toes.

'Your daughter was a twin,' said Becky's mum.

'It would explain her invisible friend,' said her dad.

'Assuming there is an afterlife,' replied my dad.

I had been a twin. My whole body tensed. There had been two of me. It made sense. A tear dribbled down my cheek. My tongue felt swollen and was stuck to the roof of my mouth.

'Your Guardian Angel,' Becky muttered. I nodded, my mind racing. You often said you were a stone, forgotten and alone in the dark. In a place we had both shared. I thought it was another lie, meant to terrify me, like the nightmares. Could a calcified foetus be a kind of stone? Because if it was, then maybe you do exist. Or did exist. Since Mummy's procedure you had been scarily silent. Where were you now? Had the doctor killed you? Is it possible to kill someone who is already dead...especially if half of them, the me part...is alive? The more I thought about it the weirder it seemed. What if I never heard from you again? It made me wish I had been nicer to you.

I had been back at school for almost a term when Mummy took me into her bedroom and sat me on the bed.

'I have a surprise,' she said. 'You're going to have a little brother or sister.'

'A sister,' I squealed. 'Oh Mummy I want a sister.'

'We have to wait and see,' she replied.

You were born two weeks before Christmas. I recognised your wrinkly, red face with the squished nose and squinty eyes from my nightmares. The screaming, your clenched fists with the weeny fingernails. If I close my eyes and concentrate I can smell the smoke, see the lilies, feel the chill beneath me...us...we are in the same body. You are my other half, my Guardian Angel and my tormentor. When I stroke your hands or touch your cheeks you seem fragile and innocent, making me want to protect you. Then I remember your meanness, your cruel teasing. Hate flares through me; I feel a strong urge to hurt you. It's confusing. If I placed my hand over your mouth, I could suffocate you, return you to the darkness. You deserve it. Only problem is, you would haunt me the same as before. Worse than before. We are bound.

Alex Yates

Alex has written several short stories, four of which are published in this second anthology of short stories from the Marion Writers Group. His primary interest is in the art of fiction and how characterisation and plotting can coalesce to produce compelling stories.

Nathan Puff's Quandary

It was Monday morning, the start of another working week, as Nathan Puff sat down for breakfast at the kitchen table. He juggled the morning newspaper in one hand and a cereal packet in the other as he cleared a space on the table to spread out the newspaper.

Ignoring the heated conversation about driving and learner's permits going on between his wife, Polly, and his teenage son, Ashley, he poured skimmed milk into his cereal bowl.

After scanning the newspaper headlines he flicked his way through the first few pages of the paper then turned to the obituary section and searched for familiar names.

This was a regular breakfast routine for Nathan who was often amazed at the number of people under 50 who had passed on from this life and into the next.

As an actuary with an insurance company he loved numbers and took every opportunity in his professional and private life to conduct 'what if' experiments with figures.

He sometimes wondered if he would reach the magical half-century, but he was in good health and took few personal risks, so taking all the relevant factors into account he figured he had a better than 97 percent chance of reaching 50.

As he perused the obituary columns, ticking off with a red marker pen the deaths of those aged below 50, he noticed a very unusual, but familiar, name—his own.

The obituary read:

PUFF, Nathan — Aged 48.

Loving husband of Polly and father of Ashley.

Passed away unexpectedly on September 5th 2013

Will be fondly remembered.

Nathan stopped chewing his cereal and read the notice again. A slight dribble of milk leaked from his lips and ran down his chin onto his light blue business shirt. He swallowed what was left in his mouth and called out. 'Look! Polly. I'm dead. It says so right here.'

Polly cut short her conversation with Ashley and turned to Nathan. 'What's wrong?' she asked.

'I think somebody's playing a joke on me.' Nathan pointed to the obituary column. 'Look!'

Polly peered over Nathan's shoulder and read the obituary. 'It must be a mistake, or an incredible coincidence,' she said. 'I thought we were the only ones with the name Puff in this State.'

'So did I,' Nathan said. 'We certainly used to be, and I can understand there being another Nathan Puff, but it's more than a coincidence that his wife's name is Polly, and he has a son named Ashley. I reckon someone's playing a joke.'

'Maybe it's somebody from your work,' Polly said. 'Somebody who doesn't like you.'

'Everybody likes me.'

Ashley giggled. 'Everybody?'

Nathan leant back in his chair. 'I'll get to the bottom of this. I'll phone the paper and find out who placed the obituary. People should have to prove to the paper who they are before the paper publishes that sort of notice.'

'Not necessarily,' Polly said.

She picked up the paper and turned to the funeral services' section. 'It says here that Nathan Puff's funeral is this afternoon at three o'clock. If you're concerned you ought to go along?'

'What about my work?'

'It's up to you. But it would be good to know what's going on.'

Nathan hesitated. 'Okay. I will.'

Nathan phoned work and told his secretary he was taking the day off. He then wandered outside to check the weather before coming back inside, removing his suit and changing into casual clothes.

After lunch he drove to the cemetery where the funeral service was to be held. When he arrived he scanned the notice boards outside the chapels for Nathan Puff's name. Unable to find it, he walked over to the office and asked the receptionist where the service for Nathan Puff was to be held.

The receptionist checked the funeral sheet for that day and looked up at him. 'I can't see the name, Puff.'

Nathan thrust the newspaper with the Births and Deaths notices in front of her and pointed to the Nathan Puff entry. She read it and checked the date. 'I think the newspaper's made a mistake,' she said. 'There's definitely no funeral for Nathan Puff today.'

Nathan felt relieved. The newspaper had got it wrong. He thanked the receptionist, turned and walked towards the door.

'However,' she said, 'by sheer coincidence, a headstone for a Nathan Puff was delivered from the engravers today. Would you like to see it?'

Nathan stopped. A cold chill rippled through his body. He reached out and grabbed a chair near the door to steady himself.

'You mean he *really* is dead?'

'Oh yes. I remember the name, Puff. It's quite an unusual name. He was buried about three months ago. Do you want to see the headstone? It's out back if you'd like to come through.'

Nathan followed the receptionist into a storeroom located behind the office. The headstone lay face up alongside some others on a runner of green carpet.

The inscription read:

NATHAN PUFF

Born: 4 — 7 — 1965

Died: 5 — 9 — 2013

Beloved husband of Polly

Father of Ashley

RIP

Nathan squatted down alongside the headstone and ran his fingers over the letters engraved in the smooth black marble. 'This could be my headstone,' he said, looking up at the receptionist. 'My name is also Nathan Puff.'

The receptionist shook her head. 'It was tragic.'

'What do you mean?'

The receptionist pointed towards two headstones alongside the Nathan Puff headstone. 'The whole family, and all on the same day.'

Nathan moved closer to the two headstones and he stooped down to read the names: Polly Puff, and Ashley Puff. On reading the names he dropped to his knees. 'This is too much of a coincidence. It must be a joke.'

'Well, if it is, someone went to quite an expense ... headstones aren't cheap.'

In his mind Nathan calculated the probability of the names being the same as those of his family.

The receptionist looked down at Nathan kneeling alongside the headstones. 'If you don't mind me saying, Puff is a very uncommon name.'

Nathan stood up. 'Yes, but what's more uncommon is that this Nathan Puff was born on the same day as me. And I also have a wife named Polly, and a son, Ashley.'

'Really!'

'Yes. Really.'

The receptionist hesitated. 'Would you like to see the graves? They're next to each other.'

Nathan took directions from the receptionist and walked by himself to the three gravesites. He stood and looked at the plots for a few minutes, trying to make sense of the whole situation. He then sauntered back to the cemetery office. 'I think I've seen enough,' he said to the receptionist. 'It's a one in a million, or even one in a trillion, coincidence.'

Nathan was confused and overcome by a need to know more about the dead man. 'Do you know where he lived?'

'Sorry, we don't keep those types of personal details. You'll have to talk to the funeral director. I can give you his phone number.'

Nathan looked at his watch. 'Okay, but I'll have to contact him tomorrow. I've had enough for now.'

Nathan tried to make sense of the events of the day as he drove away from the cemetery. When he arrived home he checked the letterbox for mail—one bill, from the electricity company. But the name on the envelope was wrong. He folded the envelope and put it in his shirt pocket and made his way to the front door. When he pushed the key into the lock, he found the key would not turn. He examined the lock and thought maybe he had inserted the wrong key. Then he tried the lock again, but was unsuccessful.

'What the hell's going on,' he muttered to himself.

He hurried around the side of the house to the back door and tried again but that door was also locked. He then checked the windows. All of them were closed. He peered through the kitchen window but did not recognise any of the furniture.

Nathan returned to the front of the house and sat on the fence near the gate. He wondered what to do. He was about to phone Polly on his mobile phone when he noticed a familiar car with a driver's 'L' plate displayed inside the front window. The car was dawdling along the street towards him. It stopped in front of the house and the passenger in the front seat wound down the window and called out to him. It was Polly.

'Ashley got his learner's licence today,' she said. 'Get in and we'll take you for a ride.'

Nathan smiled. 'Great,' He opened the door and climbed into the back seat. 'Let's go, Ash. Show us what you can do.'

As the car drove off Nathan tapped his wife's shoulder. 'Polly. You won't believe what happened today.'

Peter and His Shadow

Peter sat up in the deckchair, reached out with his right hand and, without looking, opened the ice chest. He let his hand wade around in the ice water till he felt the jagged cap of a beer bottle. He extracted the bottle and effortlessly twisted off the cap, which he then flicked back into the ice chest.

As he raised the bottle to his lips he glanced at his wife, Susan, sunbaking on a floating blow-up mattress in the middle of their backyard swimming pool.

'This is the life,' he called out, easing back into the deckchair and letting cold water run down the bottle and drip onto his hairless chest. 'I could relax like this forever.'

Susan lifted her sunglasses and looked across at him. As she studied his paunch she happened to notice his reddening skin. 'Did you use sunscreen today?'

'There wasn't any.'

'Yes there is, in the bathroom drawer ... near the shampoos and conditioners.'

'I'll put some on later.'

'Okay, but don't blame me if you end up looking like a lobster.'

Peter stood up and walked over to the pool edge. He smiled to himself as he gazed down at Susan who was paddling in slow circles.

Susan sensed his playful presence. 'Don't you dare! Go and put some suntan lotion on!'

Peter turned around and wandered into the house. A few minutes later he returned holding a white tube. 'Is this it? It says, 60+.'

'Yes, but I haven't tried it. It's supposed to be better than the other stuff, and it's non-stick. The pharmacist said one application protects you for at least a month. It contains nano-particles—whatever they are.'

Peter liberally applied the sunscreen to his face, arms, legs and body. He reached as far behind his back as he could, and even applied it to the soles of his feet. When he had finished smothering himself in the white cream he felt he had earned another beer so he visited the ice chest again. With a cold beer in one hand he walked over to the pool and slid quietly into the water and waddled towards Susan.

Susan was half asleep, enjoying the afternoon sun, when he touched her thigh with the cold bottle. 'Stop it!' she said, opening her eyes. 'I'm trying to relax.'

When she looked at Peter's face she hardly recognised him through the thick sunscreen. 'How much did you use? You're only supposed to apply a small amount, and rub it in. Didn't you read the directions?'

Peter looked at his sunscreen white arms and chest. 'It'll wash off.'

'No it won't. It's designed to stay on for at least a month. You look like you've used enough to last a year.'

'I'm sure it'll wash off.'

Peter reached out to touch Susan's exposed thighs. Sensing what he was trying to do, Susan frantically paddled backwards. 'Stay away! Don't you dare come near me! Snowman.'

Peter stood in the middle of the pool and gazed at Susan while he finished his drink. 'You're not much fun. You used to like horsing around in the pool.'

'I liked you better when you were a bronze Anzac. Thick sunscreen doesn't help your appearance.' Susan closed her eyes as she gently splashed her hot bathers and let her legs dangle in the water.

Peter threw the empty beer bottle onto the lawn. He looked around, held his nose, submerged and swam to the steps at the shallow end of the pool, climbed out and sat on the lawn. As he sat there he looked down at the grass and noticed something odd. He remained motionless for a few moments as he tried to make sense of what he saw. 'Susan, come here! Look at this! I think I'm seeing things.'

'Leave me alone, can't you see I'm resting.'

'Susan. This is important. Something's happened.'

Susan opened her eyes and slowly rotated the mattress so she was facing towards him. 'What is it? Another bee sting?'

'No, It's really strange. Come over here!'

Susan looked at Peter sitting on the lawn and paddled towards him. 'What is it, dear, a heart attack? Do you think I should call an ambulance?'

'This is serious.'

Susan rolled off the mattress into the water and swam to the edge of the pool. 'This better be good.'

Peter could not stop staring at the grass. 'Look! Here!'

Susan climbed out of the pool and looked to where Peter was pointing. 'Yes. I'm looking.'

'What do you notice?'

Susan adjusted her bathers. 'The grass?'

'No.'

'The beer bottle?'

'No.'

Peter touched the grass with his hand.

Susan gaped. 'What's happened to your shadow? I can only see the shadow of your hair and your bathers. Where's the rest?'

'That's what I'd like to know.'

Susan looked at Peter, glanced at his partial shadow on the grass, then back at him. She shook her head. 'That's weird.'

'It's that bloody suntan cream. It's done something to my skin.'

'Are you sure? Take off your bathers!'

Peter coyly lowered his bathers and turned around to expose his buttocks and upper thighs to the sun. The parts of his body not covered with suntan cream produced a shadow. He panicked. 'I've got to get this stuff off me.'

'The pharmacist said it won't wash off.'

'Well, I'm going inside to try.' Peter pulled up his bathers and ran towards the back door. He reached the bathroom and showered till the hot water ran out. He scrubbed every part of his body so hard he made his skin raw. He dried himself and ran, naked, outside, but to his dismay, where the suntan cream had been applied, there was no shadow. Feeling faint, Peter flopped into the deckchair. 'What am I going to do?'

Susan put her hand on his shoulder. 'I don't know. Maybe you should take the tube back to the pharmacist and see what he has to say.'

Peter drove to the pharmacy with the half empty tube of suntan cream and told the pharmacist what had happened. The pharmacist listened to Peter's story then followed him outside. Peter removed his shirt and revealed his partial shadow.

The pharmacist smiled. 'How much did you apply?'

'Heaps. I burn easily.'

The pharmacist read the directions on the tube and turned to Peter. 'It says to use sparingly, rub lightly into the skin until absorbed, and remove the excess.'

'But why would it affect my shadow?'

The pharmacist paused. 'It's the way it works—it uses nanotechnology. Other sunscreens work by interacting and blocking the sun's rays so they don't reach the skin. This sunscreen makes the skin transparent to the sun's rays so they pass through the skin without interacting with it. Hence, no shadow.'

'I want my shadow back the way it was.'

'You'll have to wait till the transparency effect wears off. Unfortunately, that will normally take about a month but, given the amount you've used, it might take up to a year.'

Peter frowned. He did not like the thought of being without

a shadow. 'Is there anything you can do?'

The pharmacist thought about it for a moment. 'Well, I suppose you could apply the companion tanning lotion, it's made by the same company. It's guaranteed to darken the skin and it works for about the same amount of time as the suntan cream.'

'Are there any side effects?'

'Not that I'm aware of. Anyway, all these products are thoroughly tested in the laboratory. So there shouldn't be any permanent side effects.'

Peter looked down at the ground where the shadow of his hair was bristling like a broom head without a handle. 'I suppose I'll have to give it a try. How will I know if it works?'

'Give it 24 hours. Phone me if you have any concerns.' Before leaving the pharmacy the pharmacist gave Peter strict instructions on how to apply the tanning lotion.

That evening, before bed, Peter vigorously applied the tanning lotion to his body. The next morning he rose and, naked, ran outside into the sunshine to see if his shadow had returned. When he recognised his unmistakable full shadow on the ground total relief overcame him. Excited, he called out through the bedroom window to Susan who was still in bed. 'Susan, come outside! The tanning lotion really works. I've got my shadow back.'

A minute or two later, Susan, wearing a white dressing gown over her pyjamas made her way out the back door towards the swimming pool. 'Let me see.'

Peter pointed at the ground. 'Look! My shadow's back.'

Susan gaped at Peter's shadow on the ground. 'Oh my God.' she exclaimed. 'How much tanning lotion did you use?'

'I wanted to be sure, so I used the whole jar.'

Susan cautiously outstretched her hand to touch him. 'Peter, I can see your shadow, but where are you?'

The Blood Donor

Jonas Vamp rode his red scooter past the Blood Bank building every day on his way to work. And each time he rode past the large front window of the building he glanced at the reflection of himself on his scooter. And every day he also noticed the sign painted on the window inviting him to become a blood donor. But every day as he sped past the sign he thought of reasons not to donate. What if the needle is dirty and I catch something? What if my blood is unsuitable? What if I faint? But Jonas knew, deep within himself, it was his civic duty to donate blood.

All his work colleagues donated, and they did it often, as much as three or four times a year. And if there was a blood shortage and they got a call they were quick to respond. Jonas envied them and so much wanted to be like them, to be proud and stick the small paper blood-donor badge on the lapel of his jacket. Like them, he wanted to strut around the office displaying his badge and at afternoon tea stand around the tea trolley and share stories about being a donor. He even imagined how proud he would feel to get a phone call in the middle of the night from the Blood Bank asking him to come in and donate.

Jonas did nothing about becoming a donor until one

morning, while he was busy at his desk, one of his work colleagues, a regular donor, told him the Blood Bank was offering lunch and drinks to anyone willing to donate. Only half a litre of blood was required. Although Jonas had heard that donors were offered a soft drink or a glass of beer or wine after they had donated he had never heard about food being offered. So, it was at that moment, with the generous offer of a meal, Jonas decided that the time for him to donate had come.

Later that morning, without saying where he was going, he told the office secretary he would be back late from lunch. He closed his office door, made his way to the staff car park, climbed onto his red scooter and rode, overflowing with excitement, to the Blood Bank. When he arrived he made his way to the reception area.

'I'd like to donate some blood,' he said to the receptionist. 'Is now a good time?'

The receptionist looked up at him. 'We prefer it if people book ahead, but, of course you can,' she said, reaching for a pen and a sheet of paper and handing them to Jonas. 'Did you hear about the free lunch?'

Jonas smiled at the receptionist. 'Yes.'

He held up the sheet of paper. 'What's this for?'

'It's an indemnity and medical history form. Fill out as much as you can and sign it. If you're unsure about what to write the nurse will help you.'

Jonas quickly read the form. 'When do I find out what blood type I am?'

'After we've sampled your blood,' the receptionist said. 'Fill out the form, take a seat and wait for the nurse. She'll come and get you shortly.'

As Jonas waited he looked around the walls of the reception area. Posters showing smiling donors hooked up to life-draining tubes made him question his decision. Why should I donate? he thought. There must be plenty of others willing to donate, why me? Nobody will miss my little offering. What is half a litre in what must be millions of litres of the stuff sitting in cold storage somewhere waiting to enliven the veins of those few poor souls who are running short? What if I catch an infection? He had read about donors who sued because careless nurses had used contaminated needles. As he waited he reasoned there was still time to change his mind and he was just about to get up and leave when a nurse in a white dustcoat approached him. Too late, he thought, feeling trapped. I'll have to go through with it.

The nurse introduced herself and asked him to follow her. 'It should only take about 30 minutes,' she said, 'and afterwards, you can have lunch. How does a steak, followed by some ice-cream and apple-pie, sound?'

'Great,' Jonas said. He followed the nurse out of the waiting room into a long corridor that led to a large brightly lit collection room with curtained cubicles positioned around the perimeter. From the nurses' station, an island at the centre of the room, he could observe all the cubicles, each containing a recliner chair, a bedside cupboard and an intravenous stand. All of the cubicles were occupied, except one. As Jonas was led to the vacant cubicle he noticed some of the donors were sitting back in the recliners reading or listening on headphones while others had their eyes closed, as if asleep.

Jonas removed his jacket, rolled up his left shirtsleeve, held out his exposed arm and let the nurse measure his blood pressure.

'Yep. That looks okay,' she said. Then, before he had time to question what was to happen next she pricked Jonas's little finger with a small needle.

'Ouch! What was that for?'

'We just need to check your haemoglobin levels before we get started. We don't want you to pass out on us, do we?'

Jonas said nothing. The nurse walked off with the blood sample while Jonas sat on the side of the recliner and waited till she returned.

'Yep, everything's okay', she said, smoothing out the plastic sheet covering the recliner, 'and you're blood type is a very rare strain of B negative.'

'Is that a problem?'

'No, quite the opposite. If we run short we have to ship it in from interstate but it's expensive, so we appreciate you coming in. Your blood is so rare we even pay you for being a donor.'

'Really! How much?'

'Don't get your hopes up too high, it's only a nominal amount—fifty dollars. You can pick up the money from the receptionist on your way out.'

Jonas grinned at the thought of a free lunch and fifty dollars in his pocket as well—much more than he ever expected.

The nurse attached a syringe to the end of a clear plastic tube hanging over the intravenous stand then she took hold of Jonas's arm and lightly pummelled it looking for a vein. 'Just lean back and relax,' she said.

Jonas watched all of the preparation but turned his head away just before the needle was inserted into his arm. After a few minutes he gathered enough courage to look at the syringe and the thin clear tube connected to the soft plastic bag suspended on a peg at the foot of the recliner. A nauseous feeling overcame him as he watched the deep crimson liquid wend its way down the tube into the bag. His precious blood, which was now flowing into the bag, would at some time in the future flow through someone else's veins.

The nurse returned to the island station and Jonas closed his eyes and dreamt of being back at the office with his red donor badge stuck on the lapel of his jacket and fifty dollars in his pocket. But as he lay there, thinking about how his colleagues would congratulate him back at the office, the thought of receiving fifty dollars started to make him feel uncomfortable. To be paid for donating blood seemed wrong and not really in the spirit of true giving. How could he face his work mates, who probably received nothing for their blood, knowing he had been paid to donate? No, he would refuse the money.

Twenty minutes later the plastic bag was bulging and the nurse returned to withdraw the needle from his arm. She wiped up a few drops of blood that had leaked out where the needle had been inserted and covered the punctured vein with a piece of cotton wool and an adhesive strip.

The nurse helped him stand and put on his jacket. She then felt into the top pocket of her dustcoat, pulled out a red paper badge and stuck it on his lapel. 'There. Now it's official.'

Jonas glowed inside.

'Do you feel hungry?' she asked.

Jonas smiled. 'I could eat a horse.'

'Well, come with me.' The nurse led Jonas to the donor lounge where he joined other donors who were seated at a long table. Jonas ordered his meal and while he ate and joined in their conversation he noticed their donor badges.

After lunch, but before he climbed on his scooter and returned to work, Jonas made his way back to the reception desk and with a benevolent tone of voice told the receptionist he did not want the fifty dollars.

When Jonas arrived back at work he hummed to himself as he stepped out of the lift and sauntered back to his office. Filled with excitement as he sat at his desk he found it difficult to concentrate. He was impatient waiting for afternoon tea to arrive so he could show off his badge to his colleagues. This badge would make him one of them.

At three o'clock he was first to arrive at the tea trolley. He poured himself a cup of tea and waited for the others, deciding he would say nothing, and let them notice the badge for themselves.

As each of his colleagues joined him at the trolley he made a point of saying hello, standing tall and adjusting his collar and lapel, and brushing his fingers lightly across the badge. But try as he may, he was unable to get any of them to notice it, and had almost given up, when, accidently, he brushed too hard with his fingernails and the red paper badge dislodged from his lapel and fluttered as lightly as a butterfly onto the carpet. Jonas bent down, picked it up and reattached it to his lapel.

It was only then that his colleagues noticed the badge, and understood. This was the moment Jonas had been waiting for, that precious moment when he would be inundated with congratulatory messages, hand-shakes, and questions, lots of questions: What was it like? What was his blood type? Will he donate again? Did he faint?

They listened intently as he told them of his experience. Jonas was careful not to mention the offer of fifty dollars. However, not used to being the centre of attention, Jonas felt his face turn red as he spoke. And, although he enjoyed the accolades, and felt that now he was one of them, he felt overwhelmed by their interest and he secretly wanted to be by himself, so when afternoon tea was over he was glad to get back to his office, close the door, and slump into his chair. Inundated by all the attention he had received at afternoon tea, he stared, as if in a trance, out the window at the traffic snaking its way along the freeway in the distance.

He removed the badge from his lapel and looked at it, feeling an inner pride, a satisfaction about what he had achieved that day. He had donated blood, received a free lunch, been applauded by his colleagues, and, most importantly, satisfied his desire to be truly altruistic by refusing to accept the bonus fifty dollars for having such a rare blood type.

On the way home from work that evening Jonas again looked at the reflection of himself and his scooter as he rode past the windows of the Blood Bank building. He smiled to himself as he read, once again, the sign asking for blood donors. But as the images of the day filled his memory, he was slow to notice the delivery van in front of him stop to allow a pedestrian to cross the road. By the time Jonas became aware that the van had stopped and he should apply his brakes it was too late. His scooter skidded and clipped the back of the van.

The following morning Jonas awoke to the gentle prodding of a doctor leaning over him.

Jonas, through half closed eyes, squinted at the doctor. 'Where am I?'

'Mister Vamp, you've had a road accident and you're in hospital.'

Jonas tried to understand what the doctor was saying. He recalled leaving the office and climbing onto his scooter but was unable to remember any subsequent details. 'How long have I been here?'

'The ambulance brought you in yesterday afternoon. You've had surgery.'

'My leg feels sore.'

'That's to be expected, it was broken in two places.'

Jonas looked down at his right leg. It was wrapped in plaster. 'What about my scooter?'

'Don't worry about your scooter. You're very lucky to be alive. You lost a lot of blood in the accident.'

Jonas recalled his visit to the blood bank the previous day. 'Did you know I have a rare blood type?'

'I know, and fortunately for you, just yesterday the Blood Bank took blood from a donor with your particular blood type.'

Jonas sighed. 'Serendipity, that's what it is. Serendipity. What comes around, goes around.'

The doctor sat on the edge of the bed. 'There is one other thing.'

'What's that?'

'Well, because you have such a hard-to-source blood type the Government won't subsidise the cost of the blood used for your transfusion. You'll have to pay.' The doctor placed his hand on Jonas' shoulder. 'It will cost you fifty dollars.'

The Chicken and the Egg

The magistrate struck his gavel on the sounding block and waited for the babble in the packed courtroom to subside. The court clerk pressed open a new page in his journal then pointed to a bald, middle-aged man seated in the dock. The man stood and waited for the court clerk to speak.

'Dominic De Gaulle. You are accused of causing grievous bodily harm to Humpty Dumpty by pushing him off a wall during the Grand Parade. How do you plead?'

Dominic squeezed the wooden handrail with his sweaty hands. 'Not guilty.'

The magistrate addressed Dominic. 'I notice you don't have legal representation. Do you intend to defend yourself?'

'Yes, your Honour.'

Excited chatter filled the courtroom.

'Quiet!' The magistrate waited a moment then continued. 'What is your occupation?'

'I'm a zoologist.'

'What makes you think you don't need a lawyer?'

Dominic cleared his throat. 'I studied law for a year, and I've been an expert witness in cases involving chickens.'

'Are you sure you want to represent yourself?'

'Yes, your Honour.'

The magistrate paused. 'Very well.'

'Thank you, your Honour. I can explain everything, but first I'd like to call a character witness—Christine Poulet.'

The court clerk left the courtroom and returned leading a huge, slow-moving chicken dressed in a bright yellow kaftan. At the sight of the chicken the spectator gallery erupted in laughter. The magistrate banged the sounding block and demanded quiet as the over-weight chicken hobbled into the witness box and sat down.

The magistrate turned to Dominic. 'You can't have a chicken character witness.'

'Why not?' asked Dominic. 'I don't have anyone else to call on.'

'It's unheard of.'

'But, your Honour, Christine is not a common run-of-the-mill battery hen. She's a Rhodes Scholar.'

The magistrate stroked his chin as he inspected Christine. 'Crikey. How heavy are you?'

Christine turned her head and winked at the magistrate. 'It's not polite to ask a girl how heavy she is.'

The magistrate frowned. 'Just answer the question.'

'About forty kilos.'

'Well, you're the biggest chicken I've ever seen.'

'I was part of an experimental breeding program.'

The magistrate shook his head. 'This is most irregular, but, do you, Christine Poulet, promise to tell the truth?'

'Yes, your Honour.' Christine shuffled her feathers to make herself more comfortable in the witness chair.

'How long have you known Dominic De Gaulle?'

Christine hesitated. 'About four years. You could say we met by accident.'

'How so?'

Christine looked around the courtroom then at the magistrate. 'As a chick I lived at a chicken factory. Because of the special food they fed me I became too big to be cooped up so they let me roam about the yard. Then, one day, as I was fossicking in the compost for shell grit, I met Humpty Dumpty, cleaning out the coops. It was love at first sight. Not long after that first meeting we got engaged.'

The magistrate rolled his eyes. 'Please answer the question. How did you meet Mr. De Gaulle?'

'I ran into Dominic, or should I say, he ran into me, one day as I was crossing the road. He was driving his Bantam Roadster at the time. In the accident I received concussion and a broken thighbone.'

The magistrate leaned forward. 'Can you remember why you were crossing the road?'

'Everybody asks me that. No, I can't remember.'

'Very well. Please continue.'

'So there I was, on the road, covered in blood. Fortunately, Dominic stopped and rushed over to me. He was devastated. But, to his credit, he helped me to his car and drove me to the nearest vet. And he stayed with me all night—didn't let me out of his sight.'

The magistrate put his head in his hands. 'Everybody involved in a road accident is obliged to help those who are injured ... but I don't know if that applies to injured chickens.'

Christine sobbed. 'Things didn't go well for me after the accident. Humpty Dumpty called off the engagement. He wrote me a letter saying he couldn't marry a cripple and he didn't want to see me again. I was heartbroken. Dominic was the one who helped me. He took me home with him and let me stay till I could walk.'

The magistrate shifted in his seat. 'Let's get back to this case. When did you last see Humpty Dumpty?'

'On the day of the Grand Parade.'

'Did you speak to him?'

'No, your Honour. He wouldn't speak to me, even though we raced against each other in the egg and spoon race.'

The magistrate raised his eyebrow. 'You, a chicken, raced against an egg? Doesn't that give you an unfair advantage?'

'No, your Honour, Humpty's a great athlete. He's won the egg and spoon race for the last three years in a row.'

The magistrate pushed his fingers through his grey hair. 'Did you see Dominic on the wall next to Humpty Dumpty during the Grand Parade?'

'Yes.'

'Why was he on the wall?'

'He wanted to tell Humpty about the Competition.

'What competition?'

'It might be better if Dominic explains the Competition to you.'

The magistrate threw his arms in the air. 'This is hopeless. I didn't pass the bar exam to listen to an overweight chicken tell me about an egg and spoon race and her failed love life.' He signalled for the court clerk to help Christine leave the witness box. 'Let's hear what Mr. De Gaulle has to say.'

Christine stepped down and waddled her way to a seat at the back of the courtroom. The court clerk then called Dominic De Gaulle to the witness box.

The magistrate addressed Dominic. 'I can't see what Miss Poulet's testimony has to do with you pushing Humpty Dumpty off the wall.'

'Your Honour, I didn't push him. He slipped.'

'What were you doing on the wall?'

'Telling him about the Great Omelette Competition. The person who can make the world's biggest omelette with one egg will be given a king's ransom.'

The magistrate crossed his arms. 'What does the Great Omelette Competition have to do with Humpty Dumpty?'

'With respect, your Honour, I think it is obvious. You can't make an omelette without breaking an egg, and Humpty is the world's biggest egg.'

The magistrate sighed.

Dominic continued. 'After the egg and spoon race Christine overheard a European chef talking about a plot to kidnap Humpty after the Grand Parade, so I climbed the wall to warn him. That's when I spotted Christine in the crowd talking to one of the King's men. Humpty wanted to call her over and hear directly from her what she had heard about the Competition, so

205

we both stood up and waved to her.'

'I thought Humpty Dumpty wasn't talking to her.'

'He wasn't, but he wanted to hear first hand about the plot. That's when he lost his balance and fell. I tried to grab him but his shell was covered in suntan lotion and he slipped through my fingers. The next I knew his head was splattered all over the footpath. You could see all the yolk oozing out. It was awful.'

'So, if it was an accident, why did you run away?'

'I was standing next to him on the wall. I thought people wouldn't understand.'

'What makes you think I believe you?'

'But it's the truth, your Honour.'

'You'll have to produce more evidence than that to convince the Court.'

'I will, your Honour. I would like to call Humpty Dumpty to the witness box.'

The chatter in the courtroom reached a crescendo.

'Quiet!' the magistrate yelled, then continued. 'Didn't Humpty Dumpty suffer severe brain damage?'

'Yes, your Honour, but one of the King's men is a neurosurgeon and he patched him up. He's expected to make a full recovery.'

'Well, that's good news.'

The court clerk left the room and returned with Humpty Dumpty in a wheelchair. Humpty's head was wrapped in a cotton bandage with slits for his eyes, mouth and ears. The court clerk assisted Humpty Dumpty into the witness box.

The magistrate waited for the witness to settle. 'Humpty

Dumpty, can you explain to the Court why you were on the wall?'

'I was watching the Grand Parade.'

'And did Mr. De Gaulle sit along side you.'

'Yes.'

'Did you invite him to sit with you?'

'No. He came up to me, sat down and told me about the Great Omelette Competition. He said that at the end of the egg and spoon race, Christine, my ex fiancé, had heard about a plot to kidnap me and use me to make the world's biggest omelette.'

'Then what happened?'

'I didn't believe him at first, but when I thought about it I became anxious and wanted to ask Christine if it was true.'

'I thought you weren't talking to her.'

'I wasn't. But she's the one who heard about the plot. Anyway, Dominic pointed her out in the crowd so we both stood up to wave and beckon her over.'

The magistrate leaned back in his chair. 'Have you spoken to her since falling off the wall?'

'No, your Honour, and I'm sorry. I've been a self-centred egghead. I rejected her when she was injured and needed me most. Now I know how she felt.' A tear slipped through the slit in Humpty's bandage. 'While I was in hospital I had time to think about her and what in life really matters. I now realise that I love her and I hope she can find it within herself to take me back.'

'The Court is not interested in your on-again off-again relationship with Ms Poulet. Did Mr. De Gaulle push you?'

'No, your Honour. When I waved to Christine I slipped. He tried to grab me as I fell but on an eggshell there's not much to hold on to.'

The magistrate closed his folder and slumped in his chair. 'The case against Mr. De Gaulle is dismissed.'

Loud cheers erupted in the courtroom. Christine rose from her seat and shuffled over to Humpty Dumpty to embrace him. Humpty Dumpty told her he was sorry and kissed her beak. As they left the courtroom, they held hands for the photographers.

Within a minute only the magistrate and Dominic remained in the courtroom.

'Dominic. I have one further question about this year's egg and spoon race.'

'Yes, your Honour?'

'Who came first, Christine Poulet or Humpty Dumpty?'

Dominic smiled. 'I never did find out, your Honour.'

Athena Zaknic

Athena started writing after retiring from pharmacy a few years ago.Her preferred genres are memoir and poetry which includes free verse and Japanese genres. Some of her poems and short stories have been published in various anthologies in Australia and overseas. Athena is a member of the Bindii Japanese genres group and an active member of U3A at the Box Factory. Other interests include learning languages, classical music, reading, and going to the theatre and movies.

Ariadne's story

It was one of those late autumn afternoons, when everything seems to fulfil its role perfectly. Or so it seemed to Ariadne who had left work earlier than usual on that day. With time to spare before she met friends for a movie, she decided to go for a sprint towards the Botanical Gardens. She lived in South Yarra, an inner leafy Melbourne suburb, in privileged proximity to the CBD.

With legs flexed in her new fluorescent lime green sneakers she seemed to bounce off the freshly mowed grass bordered with glorious flowering hydrangeas. A few crisp autumn leaves here and there completed a canvas worthy of an artist's brush. A long line of palms lined the southern walls of the Gardens. They murmured in unison with the approaching westerly.

Now inside the gardens, Ariadne jogged towards the central lake. As a child she was often brought there for a picnic by her family. They always aimed to sit near the lake with the black swans, which no one was allowed to feed. It was unusually quiet, with no one else around. As she turned into the narrow path leading toward the lake, a magnificently marked cat jumped in front of her. Ariadne startled, side stepped to avoid the animal.

She noticed a green velvet ribbon around its neck. Ariadne assumed the animal must be female. Surely no male cat could be so beautiful.

Above its long whiskers emerald sparks flashed from two exotic eyes. It was a green scene all around, including Ariadne with the green sneakers, and the green eyed cat with the green ribbon around its neck. Ariadne wondered if green was supposed to be a lucky colour. The cat followed her as they approached the large lake formation. There were five black swans floating majestically on the calm murky waters.

Contrary to the forecast, gathering clouds, now a dense grey, suddenly exploded. Soon small pools of water filled cavities on the ground. Ariadne rushed to take refuge in a concrete hexagonal shelter close by. She was surprised to see the cat perched on the concrete bench running around its walls. A feeling of déjà-vu gripped Ariadne. Mesmerised she stared into the two fluorescent jewels opposite her. They both sat and waited for the downpour to stop. Finally when it cleared, and the sun had returned, Ariadne went outside following the cat. She looked around for it, but could not see it.

As the sun started to set, Ariadne decided to head for the coffee shop in Marne Street. A large hot espresso would restore her equilibrium.

As she was walking out of the South entrance of the Botanical Gardens, she heard someone playing a familiar tune on a piano. A few seconds after a flash of lightning struck. The music was coming from across the road. It was right then when Ariadne saw her ginger friend dart past her almost knocking her over. She swiftly followed the cat out of the gardens and saw it leap up the wall of an apartment directly opposite. In the fading day-light, Ariadne noticed a dilapidated art deco façade.

Again she heard the familiar sound of Rachmaninoff's second piano concerto. It was the piece she had studied at school in music appreciation. She looked up to the first floor at the open window and she saw the cat disappear inside. Ariadne determined to find out more, marched towards the front gate. She pulled the heavy iron handle just as a voice from behind startled her.

'No one has lived here for years.' She turned around and was surprised to see an old man with a long grey beard and a black hat. He belongs to some religious order, Ariadne thought.

'Why would that be?' She asked. 'This is a very sought after area.'

'The owners moved overseas years ago. They are not interested in selling it,' he said quietly. Ariadne suspected he knew a lot more.

'Who is playing the piano then?' Ariadne asked. The Rachmaninoff was now in its second movement.

'You can hear him play?' The old man's eyes widened as he stroked his beard.

'Yes,' replied. 'Can't you?'

'Today, with the thunder, you can hear Sergei play.' His eyes clouded for an instant and his mouth contracted into an ominous smile.

Ariadne had to find out more. She must know. It was as if her life depended on it. The cat had told her that inside the gardens.

She had understood it perfectly.

'What has happened to him? Is he still here?'

'You don't understand. Sergei was killed 20 years ago.'

Ariadne stepped closer to hear him better. The rain had eased. He continued softly. 'The bullet that killed Sergei was fired on the seventh of May. It was a night of thunder and lightning, like today. You did say you heard the piano just now?' He looked at her with misgiving.

'Yes. The Rachmaninoff second piano concerto. Tell me about the day he died.'

He noticed the urgent tone in her voice, and smiled. 'No one heard the shot. His cat was beside him when the cleaners found him the next day.'

'Did Sergei have a family?' She felt compelled to find out whatever there was to know.

'No, only his cat.'

'What sort of cat was it?' Ariadne felt moist beads of perspiration on her neck.

'Her fur was a mottled shade of gold and she had beautiful green eyes. Militza was the most beautiful animal I have ever seen. He loved her like a best friend, even more than that.' He stopped to wipe his eyes. 'It is rumoured he was able to speak with her. That is not at all surprising now, is it young lady?'

'Why should it be?' Ariadne felt a long shiver crawl up her spine.

'It is said that relationships between humans and animals can be closer than one may think possible'.

'Has anyone seen this cat again?'

'I don't know. No one as far as I know. It was a long time ago.' He raised his hand, almost as if to give her a blessing, and started to walk away.

She smiled and extended her hand, which he squeezed gently. For a few seconds she felt his long bony fingers wrapped around her small hand. It was a weird feeling.

Nightfall shrouded him as he walked away, and Ariadne all alone once more, gulped a few long breaths to clear her head. She decided to jog slowly towards the café in Marne Street, with comforting thoughts of a hot espresso and a piece of Black Forrest cake. A reward for her endurance of the past two hours. Did I not hear music and did I not see that cat? My wild Imagination is at it again. She kept talking to herself as she increased her pace.

That night Ariadne slept unusually soundly, and her days at work after the experience in the gardens assumed a purpose, which up till now had been absent.

A few days later Ariadne walked back to the same spot outside the gardens opposite the old apartments, where she had heard the music, to see what would happen. Nothing did, so she decided to forget all about it for a while.

Three months later during a bout of torrential rain, she felt compelled to try again. Although it was late at night, she went out wrapped in a long plastic raincoat. She approached the wall of the gardens just as a bolt of lightning lit up the sky. Bravely she waited outside, across the road from the apartment where she heard the piano. Simultaneously, a second more severe flash of lightning slashed the sky as the piano was heard playing the same piece as before.

Ariadne was mortally knocked down as the Rachmaninoff chords thundered across the road. It was a minute past midnight. A ginger cat approached her lifeless body and licked her warm cheeks.

It was the seventh of May, Ariadne's 21st birthday, 21 years since the fatal shot was fired. No one heard Sergei play again. He had finally found his soul mate.

Just coffee

The old lady shuffled under the bedcovers, and listened to her grandson read...

'Some of her vital organs were spread on the mortuary table for examination. The mortician had never encountered anything like this before. He called in another colleague to help him evaluate this unusual incident.

They eventually came to the conclusion that her organs were severely damaged as a result of a cataclysmic orgasm.'

'She must have just gone out at the height of it,' the younger man said. He turned to his older colleague, who promptly replied, 'Cardiac arrest was the precipitator, so she probably did not suffer at all. It would have been instantaneous. This came about after she had consumed 13 cups of a special organic coffee from Columbia.'

'Did you like your bedtime story, Granny?' The young lad gently prodded the old lady's ribs as she turned in her bed to look at him.

'Very much.' A ghastly grin spread from ear to ear on her deeply creviced face.

'Do you know where I can get some of that coffee?' She got up slowly, walked towards the west windows, and pressed a button on the window frame. This rendered a dull orange shade to the glass, which subdued the influx of the afternoon sun.

An odious smile shaped his thin lips and he nodded his shaved head, glistening mirror-like in the bright sun. With his tattooed arm on the old lady's shoulder, he gave her a nudge and a wink. She winked back.

'I can order some for you. It will only take a couple of days.'

'Marius, would you bring me my wallet from the second drawer and then put the mastevision on channel 51? I will request the orchestra play 'The dance of the fairies'. Faustus Klein promised to play it on my 102nd birthday tomorrow. In 2013, when I was born, you could not make requests like this. But then no one lived over 100. How times have changed!' A croaky laugh left her hoarse throat and resounded on the glass that formed the walls on three sides of the room.

The lad picked up his fluorescent backpack from the silver swivel chair and headed for the door.

'Thanks for the extra cash Granny. Your coffee should be here in a few days. And remember, you must only drink a little bit at a time.' She could not see the smirk on his face as he opened the door. She heard the roar of his motorcycle as he sped away, to meet up with his mob.

Ten minutes later Marius entered the bowling alley where his friends hung out every afternoon. He approached a tall well-built man about twenty years of age, who was at that moment vigorously stirring a pink frothy concoction that had a strong smell of vanilla and alcohol. He was wearing thigh boots and had his legs stretched on the low table in front of him. His sleeveless leather vest, studded with metal, hung loosely over tight black leather pants. He lifted his arms and nodded at the newcomer.

'What have you been up to now Marius? We've been here over an hour.' He pointed his heavily ringed finger at the newcomer, as a statement of his authority. The four other men cackled and nodded their partly shaved heads in unison.

'I need two grams of the stuff by Friday, Morgan.'

'Two Gs? Have you won the lottery, Marius, or what?'

'I will soon have all the money I owe you, and much more.' He placed three large purple notes on the table.

Morgan picked them up, and after holding them up to the light he put them in his pocket. 'You'll get it by Friday next week. The shipment is coming from Burma and its purity is guaranteed this time.'

Back home the old lady dug her bony fingers into the silver grey Persian cat's luxuriant neck. 'Now my precious, don't forget to thank my blessed nephew in your prayers tonight. He has just assured your future. I can hear my beloved Homer calling me to join him. You remember Homer, my precious, don't you? How he searched for you, as a gift for my very special birthday two years ago. Just before that nasty disease snatched him from us.'

With these words she picked up her star-shaped wonder phone, and pressed the blue button twice to see and speak to Aloysius Grantly, her good friend and solicitor of many years.

The Egyptian artefact

I still have time to plant the seedlings, I'm not due at Marianne's till 2.00 pm. Anita was keen to try growing a few vegetables. Marianne, a hairdresser and her best friend and confidante, worked from home. Anita would have a haircut and then a long chat over coffee.

In her gardening attire with gloves and a large brimmed hat, Anita walked to the allocated veggie patch, picked up her shovel and started to dig. Best to aerate the soil well, before planting, the garden experts had advised her. The plan was to grow three varieties of tomatoes. Something she had tried before without success.

The clear spring sky suddenly filled with grey clouds. A few drops of rain at first, then a downpour. The soil became indented with deep puddles. Just as Anita decided to stop digging, she felt a hard object resisting her shovel. Curious, she defied the rain, and in a few minutes she had excavated a small metal tin about 20cm long by 10cm wide. I wonder what is inside, she thought, as she tried to force open the rusted lid. At that moment she heard footsteps on the back veranda and saw her husband walking towards her.

'Frank, have a look at this,' she called out. Without a word he took the tin from her and walked back to the shelter of the veranda. Anita, totally drenched by now, followed him.

'I wonder what's inside?' she whispered.

'You better get some dry clothes on first, then we'll get to this.'

Anita soon returned wearing a purple tracksuit. She hadn't bothered to dry her hair.

'Okay, let's open the damned thing,' Frank muttered.

After a brief struggle he forced the heavily rusted lid open. Both held their breaths as he slowly took out an envelope. Anita grabbed it from him and tore it open. Inside was a faded black and white photograph wrapped in a sheet of paper that looked like some sort of a map. 'What does it all mean?' she asked.

Frank first shrugged his shoulders, and then with a sneer in his voice turned to his wife. 'A treasure hunt perhaps! Still I wouldn't get too excited. You may still need your tomatoes yet.' How bloody patronising, Anita thought. She stood up and announced she was making a hot cup of tea. This was one of the last remaining rituals they still shared. Most of the other marriage accoutrements had fallen away or more correctly were pushed away by both of them. Anita phoned Marianne and cancelled her hair appointment. More important matters were at hand now.

The rain subsided. The sun's rays re-appeared. Steeped in thought they sat on the veranda sipping their tea. After a few minutes Frank picked up the excavated sheet of paper and studied it once again. 'It looks like some type of map. I wonder who drew it? And what the hell is it doing in our garden?' Anita looked at it briefly, then concentrated on the photograph. 'Look, Frank, there is a row of cypress trees along the back fence, and there are two bay trees, one on each side of the shed. What does that remind you of?'

'Yes, you're damn right' he said, taking a closer look at the photograph. 'It looks like your grandmother's garden in the Adelaide hills.'

'Remember we used to visit her quite often after grandfather died.' Anita tried to think back to the days when as a young married couple they would drive to her grandmother's house to keep the old lady company for a few hours.

'Didn't your grandmother tell you a strange story about her husband, Hugo, and his adventures as a young man?' Frank asked.

'Yes, it is all coming back to me,' Anita replied.

'Wasn't he in some sort of war?' Frank asked with interest. Anita stopped for a few seconds to recall what she knew about her grandfather's early life.

'He was in his early twenties when he joined the Foreign Legion. There were rumours about his past. No one knew much about him and the mystery surrounding him remained with him.'

'I never knew much about him,' Frank said, as he leaned forward. 'Go on.'

'It was reported that he had been wounded fighting in Egypt close to an archaeological site, during a sandstorm. It was just outside the great Pyramid of Giza. After he recovered, it was believed that he returned home with something to which he had no right to. As a child I often heard grandmother relate this story. She said it was half-truth and half-myth. Like himself, secrecy was at the heart of the tale.' Anita poured herself a second cup, and then continued. 'As I remember, it sounded like it may have been some sort of an artefact.'

'What was it, and what happened to it?' Frank was getting quite excited.

'No one knows. He kept it well hidden. I never heard grandmother, mother, or anyone else mention having ever seen it. It was never seen by anyone, as far as I know.'

'Why all the secrecy?' Frank's voice was getting louder.

'I guess he would have been charged with robbery, which it was.' Anita put her cup down and picked up the chart again.

'I assumed it may have been some sort of a vase or small statue or even jewellery. It could not have been anything bulky. He would have had to carry it on him.'

'This thing, whatever it is, could be worth quite a lot,' Frank remarked. He jumped off his chair and started pacing the floor his palms pressed together as if in prayer.

'I guess so. A small fortune, perhaps?'

She paused a minute. Frank thought her cheeks now looked like the tomatoes she was hoping to grow.

'I say, Frank, you don't suppose ...?

'Do you remember who bought the house after your grandmother died?' Frank cut in.

'I am not quite sure. I think they were Italians. I wonder if they are still there. They have probably left by now.'

Over the next few days Frank made inquiries about

Grandmother's house. It now belonged to a retired police sergeant. He was a widower and lived there on his own.

'How can we ask him to let us dig around his house for something that doesn't legally belong to us?' Frank asked his wife.

'Belongs to me, you mean.' Anita was quick to answer. 'She was my grandmother you know.'

Frank's chalky face took on a rosy hue. 'What is yours is mine. Isn't that what marriage is all about?'

Anita got off her seat and faced him. 'Well then, how is it you decided to sell the Aston Martin your uncle had left you, without mentioning anything to me?' As she spoke, her dark eyes pinned his with the intensity of a bird of prey.

Frank crossed his arms, and stood there silently, facing the barrage with valour, as he had been well rehearsed in scenes like these in the past.

'One day we had a family vintage car which we proudly drove annually at the Southern Rally. Remember? The next day you came home with a worthless pile of stamps. Oh yes, you also bought me a bunch of flowers. Red roses when you know I prefer yellow.'

He had heard all this before whenever they disagreed, which was happening more and more lately. How he had wished there were no such things as yellow roses. His wife would never forgive him for that misdemeanour.

'I don't mind you spending hours over your stamps, Frank, but you could have asked me how I felt about selling that car.' He wished her shrill tone would not stress him as much as it did.

After arguments like this she would go to Marianne's house where she usually stayed the night. He now anticipated this happening.

'When I complained about the car,' she continued, 'you said it was yours to do with as you pleased. Remember Frank?'

'What is all this leading to Anita? Are you trying to tell me that if you ever manage to get your hands on your grandmother's artefact or whatever it is, you will cut me out of the millions it may fetch?' She ignored him and rushed to draw the curtains, to keep their raised voices within the confines of the room. Frank confronted her, his face as ruddy as it would ever get. 'Just because I sold the car without telling you?'

They pounded each other with the marital issues they had sown over the years, laying bare the thin veneer of their marriage. Then Frank, suddenly, without a word got up, and grabbed his overcoat and hat. He slammed the door behind him as he went out into the night leaving Anita in a high state of excitement and shock.

When she managed to calm down, she thought about her husband's not so unexpected reaction. Concluding he had left her for good, she grabbed the contents of the box and with a weird smile, tore them into shreds. Then she made herself a cup of tea, picked up the phone and made a long distance call to Rio de Janeiro. It was answered by Sergeant Ted Meadows formerly of the Adelaide Hills.

Travis James &
Haydn Radford

A collaboration.

Alien 1

Waiting at the traffic lights, Constable Anne Parker sat in the driver's seat of the unmarked police vehicle. Along with Senior Constable Steve Brooks, they observed the hookers on the corner soliciting the drivers cruising by. Other girls of the night mingled with the passing foot traffic moving towards the clubs, pubs and strip joints. Word was around there was a new supplier of crystal meth in town. This had resulted in more emergency admissions to local hospitals, along with an increase in armed robberies on soft targets such as petrol stations and small shops.

Parker watched pedestrians stream across the intersection. She desperately needed something to happen to break the tedium. Her recent transfer to the Drug Squad had been her foremost goal since joining the force. With the recent increase in ice related crimes she considered this her big chance to make a strong impression with her supervisor.

A blue Porsche 911 pulled up alongside; its deep gurgling exhaust throbbed as the driver repeatedly tapped the accelerator.

'Well hello, what do we have here? It looks like my prayers have been answered,' Parker thought. She looked at the dark tinted windows, which concealed the driver. 'Well Steve, here's a violation if I ever saw one. Time for us to have a meet and greet.'

Parker pressed the horn to attract the driver's attention, and signalled for the driver to pull over. The traffic lights changed to green and both cars began to move forward across the intersection with the other vehicles. There was an opening in the traffic. The Porsche's rumbling exhaust increased to a deafening roar followed by a deep bark; black smoke erupted from its spinning rear wheels as the car zig-zagged between the other vehicles.

'Hey! What the hell!' yelled Parker. She switched on the siren and proceeded after the Porsche amidst a stream of traffic.

Three cars screeched to a halt to avoid colliding with the Porsche. What followed was a succession of bangs, as a line of vehicles crumpled together in a chain collision, creating a major traffic jam. 'Shit! Let's go get him.' Brooks reached out the window positioning the flashing light on the roof. Parker weaved her vehicle through the traffic and once clear, she accelerated. Up ahead the Porsche could be seen speeding ahead of the traffic.

'How do you know the driver's a he?' When Brooks didn't answer, Parker tried again, only louder. 'You said, "him", before. What makes you think it's a male driver?'

Brooks shrugged. 'It was just a turn of phrase.'

'You guys are all the same. You think you are the only ones who can drive at high speed.'

'Oh not again. You can cut the sexist crap...just keep after the little shit will ya.' Brooks ordered. 'Just don't lose him...her... Did you get his...her... fucking number?'

She took a deep breath. 'Alien1.'

'You've gotta be joking?' He slowly shook his head.

'I'm not,' grinned Parker.

'Well don't let this little Trekkie get away...let's go get ourselves an alien,' said Brooks tightening his seat buckle. He clutched the handle above the door. Memories of wrecked cars mangled together with dead and injured when a drunk driver cannonballed through an intersection hitting four cars and killing two women. He was the first on the scene. The screams of the injured still haunted him. He pressed the button on the radio microphone. 'Control. Car 172.'

'Car 172.' Control replied.

'Car 172. We have a major accident near the intersection of Main Road and Bonython Road. We are pursuing a blue Porsche 911, Registration Alien 1. Current estimated speed one hundred plus.' Who names a car Alien 1, he thought as he waited for a response.

'Car 172. Pursuit authorised. Do they need ambulances at scene?' asked Control.

'Car 172, not sure, but suggest one attend.'

'They will need a few tow trucks.' Parker yelled. She was trying her best, but their patrol car wasn't a pursuit vehicle, just a finely tuned domestic. She cursed the communication equipment in the boot weighing the car down. Her motor rally experience kicked in. She dropped the gears back and planted her foot. They gradually gained a little on the Porsche. The two cars weaved through the traffic as if in formation. Some of the other motorists braked suddenly. A few just slowed down. Others obviously shaken, pulled over to the kerb to get clear. Parker navigated around other vehicles, keeping her cool.

'Car 172, it's Sergeant Gamblin. Please confirm the car registration you are pursuing is Alien 1.'

Brooks responded. 'Car 172, licence plate is Alien 1.'

'Car 172, you are not, I repeat, not to apprehend the driver of Alien 1. Is that clear Car 172? Over.'

'What? Car 172. He's doing over a hundred down Main Road, and you don't want us to arrest him ...this Alien 1?'

'Car 172, I repeat you are not to make contact with the driver of Alien 1. Do not apprehend until otherwise instructed. Understood car 172? Over.'

'Yes, Control,' said Brooks. He said with a shrug. 'This Gamblin is new to me. Have you come across him before?'

'No,' she replied, shaking her head. 'Perhaps he's new to Traffic Division.'

The Porsche sped towards a busy intersection. The red lights unexpectedly turned green causing bedlam with vehicles braking and swerving to avoid collisions. The Porsche manoeuvred through narrowly missing the other vehicles. Parker attempted to follow, but the traffic lights changed to red. She braked heavily, her tyres screeching as she stopped short of colliding with a utility, which swerved and collided with a small sedan.

'Fuck! Did you see that? Parker snapped. 'It's as if the lights changed earlier, to stop us.'

The Porsche continued along the highway.

Brooks reached for the microphone. 'Car 172, calling Control.' No response. He repeated himself, only much louder. 'Car 172, calling Control...'

There was a shrill whistling followed by a crackling sound over the radio 'Car 172, just maintain your position behind the Porsche, registration Alien 1. Do not apprehend. Over.'

'That sounds like that Gamblin again...What do you make of him?' asked Brooks turning to Parker, who just shook her head. Obviously just as mystified. 'It's not normal procedure for two Operations Officers to be giving us instructions.'

'I'm with you, there is something weird going on here,' she replied. 'Why don't we just tail this Alien 1 and see what happens.'

'Okay. But not too close. I don't want Gamblin to get wind of what we're doing.'

The Porsche turned up the hills highway and powered away. Parker flattened the accelerator. A quick glance at the rev counter showed the needle was in the red. They needed everything the car could give just to maintain sight of the Porsche. Parker maintained maximum revs.

Brooks clutched the handle above the door. 'Anne there's no shame if he or she gets away you know. Besides it won't go down well for us if we're involved in an accident. There's enough shit goin' down with that patrol chasing that stolen BMW, which wrapped itself around a tree. A sixteen year old passenger was killed and the driver's in intensive care.'

'It's okay Brooksie, relax will ya. We're not going to crash,' said Parker, with a hint of a smile.

'Bloody hell! You're actually enjoying this. You're crazier than I thought.' He sighed as he studied her face. 'And another thing, it's Brooks, not Brooksie.'

Both cars continued at high speed along the multi-lane highway through the hills. Where the highway changed from three lanes to two, and surrounding areas are open grazing properties and pasture paddocks, the Porsche did a sharp right turn, its high beam lighting up a single dirt road. Its red tail lights glowed like bloodshot eyes in the pitch darkness. Parker turned to follow but the police car slid sideways running over small bushes on the verge on the corner.

'S-h-i-t!' said Brooks, clutching the grip as if his life depended on it. Parker eased back on the pedal, manoeuvred the car onto the middle of the road, holding it steady. Planting her foot she pursued the diminishing tail lights of the Porsche.

'Steve, whoever the driver is, you've gotta agree he or she's bloody good.'

'You're unbelievable. This is not one of your rallies, you know?' He looked tense. His rising anxiety noticeable in his tone of voice.

Parker laughed. 'I'm unbelievable? Have you ever considered a career change?'

'Car 172, this is Control, I will instruct PolAir to assist you.'

'Car 172, Thanks Control. Control what's with this Alien 1?' Asked Brooks.

'Car 172. Vehicle Porsche, Alien 1 is registered to that young pro-tennis player, who calls himself Zorba the Great. He was in trouble last year over a drugs scandal and was mixing with a wild crowd. What is strange, officers have checked and have reported his car was not stolen. They sighted it at his home on the Gold Coast. What's the situation with that Porsche, Car 172?'

'Control, we're doing as instructed, we're holding back.'

'Car 172, what do you mean, you're holding back?'

'Control, we're following orders from Sergeant Gamblin. He told us not to impede the Porsche.' 'What? Not again... Car 172, there's no Sergeant Gamblin here. For your info, Traffic Control HQ complained earlier of interference with radio transmissions and the traffic lights. It appears a hacker is creating confusion on our frequency. Car 172, we need you to resume the chase after Alien 1 and you are to arrest the driver.'

'Yes Control.'

The hunt was on again. Parker and Brooks looked at one another. She grinned. Brooks was struck by her resemblance to a fox pursuing its favourite prey. The vehicle bounced repeatedly as it hit mounds of dirt and overshot the corner ploughing through clumps of saltbush. Parker jammed on the brakes. The car stopped. She spun the tyres as she reversed to the turn-off. As she planted her foot the heavy police vehicle zig-zagged along the dirt road.

'Car 172, Are you still there?'

'That's debatable,' answered Brooks. 'In the distance we can see the tail lights of the Porsche.'

'Car 172, PolAir will be with you shortly. Meanwhile continue tracking Alien 1.'

The two cars stirred the dust high into the darkness as they raced along the dirt road. Finally the Porsche slowed down as if searching for something. Its headlights focused on a closed gate. Then at high speed it crashed through leaving the gate mangled and dangling loosely.

'Shit! Did you see that? What a nutter,' yelled Brooks. He turned and looked out the passenger window on hearing what sounded like something circling overhead. Glancing back at Parker, he saw that fixed look in her eyes, and that wry smile he was beginning to recognise all too well.

'Oh no...'

'Hold on Brooksie.'

'You'll have us both sentenced to desk jobs if you're not careful.'

They hit a run of corrugations that sent ripples through the car and its occupants.

'Whoops, sorry.'

'Steve this will be the-ride-you'll-tell-your-grand-kids-about.' She laughed out loud.

'If-I'm-still-alive.' They hit another deep furrow. His head hit the ceiling. 'Oh-shit!' Brooks grabbed hold of the safety handle.

Sensing the funny side, Parker burst into song. *'Good, good, good, good vibrations. She gives me excitations.'*

'Oh, very funny.'

'Perhaps you'd prefer...*This could be the last time, this could be the last time, maybe the last time.*' Singing in full voice she maintained maximum pressure on the accelerator. They rocketed forward, bouncing through the gateway and across the field swerving to and fro, as did the Porsche, both cars veering side to side on the slippery stubble in the furrowed field.

'Maybe the last time...I don't know...' continued Parker in full voice. There was no stopping her now as they headed up a slight rise of open ground. The Porsche's brake lights lit up. It stopped.

A young woman dressed in a shiny silver body suit climbed out of the Porsche clutching a package. She stepped in front of the vehicle looking upwards as if to attract someone's attention. Her striking long flowing blonde hair glowed in the Porsche's headlights.

'Who'd she be meeting out here,' asked Brooks. And then all of a sudden there was his answer. Above them, a beam of white light shone down, rotating slowly in circles, scanning the area. Parker braked. The vehicle stopped. Brooks stretched out the open passenger door window trying to see where the light was coming from. 'That can't be PolAir. What the hell...' He couldn't believe what he was seeing. It was definitely not the Police helicopter. A spaceship hovered over-head. Brooks reached for the radio handset. His voice trembled. 'Control 172, calling Control.' No answer. Shouting his time. 'Car 172, calling Control. This is an emergency! Fuck is there anyone there!' Still no response.

Brooks heard the click as Parker's car door opened. She stepped from the car and ran towards the woman. 'What do you think you're doin'?' he called out to Parker.

'Car 172, Gamblin here, you were instructed not to pursue the Porsche.'

Brooks watched Parker approaching the young woman.

'Car 172, I'm ordering you to stand down. Immediately.' Gamblin said.

'Screw you,' yelled Brooks. He disconnected the call. 'What in the hell are you doing Parker?' he called out. 'Get back here.'

He got out of the car, and watched Parker as she moved

slowly towards the young woman who was now encircled by a beam of white beam. The young woman stood still looking upwards.

'Parker, stay where you are,' yelled Brooks. But she either didn't hear him, or wasn't listening. She just continued to creep closer towards the young woman.

A gold beam emerged from the craft, lowering an older man. He was quite short, but stood with his hands on his hips, and exerted an air of authority... But what caught Brook's attention was the man's blue hair and long pointed ears. As the man landed, the young woman still clutching the package hesitantly approached him. When she was about three metres from him, she saluted him. He held up his open hand clearly indicating for her not to come any closer. She began pleading with him. He gestured angrily and shouted at her.'

'That voice...' uttered Brooks. 'That sounds like Gamblin.' The man continued his tirade. Clutching the package under one arm she reached up with her other hand and pulled off a wig to show very close cropped blue hair and her pointed ears.

'Parker stand down! It is not safe,' yelled Brooks.

The man turned towards Parker pointing a finger at her and then Brooks. Parker froze not knowing quite what to do. She looked back to the patrol car. Brooks stood by the vehicle. He was still holding the radio handset, and appeared to be trying talking into it. His hand gestures conveyed to Parker he was having problems with the radio. Clearly frustrated Brooks let go of the microphone and reached for his pistol. He started to move towards her. Parker watched the young woman slump to her knees. She was sobbing as she pleaded with the man, who continued his tirade.

'...due to your careless actions they know we are here.' 'Give me one more chance... please. I will put things right,' she cried.

'How can you possibly do that?' He looked at Parker, aware she was witnessing everything. He turned to the young woman.

"Because of your foolish actions they now know we are here.' He reached out his hand. 'Give me the package.'

Reluctantly the woman handed the package to him. He ripped it open, examined it closely and sniffed the contents.

'You not only duplicated an Earthling's vehicle, but you also tampered with the bio-variant crystals, to create this illicit drug.' Clearly enraged he moved towards her, shouting furiously and pointing at her and the package. He showed no interest in what she tried to say. All at once, she attempted to grab the package from him. He pulled back, turning away from her, but as they struggled with the package, the clear chunky crystals scattered on the ground. Crying out loud, she fell upon the crystals and desperately attempted to gather them. The old man watched her scooping them up with her fingers. He shook his head looking deeply saddened by her behaviour.

He produced what appeared to be a hand gun and pointed it at the woman. She raised her hands in defence, begging for mercy. A bright light followed by a shrill sound. She screamed. Then silently she rose to her feet and stepped slowly into the gold beam. He raised one hand and appeared to speak into something attached to his wrist. A green beam flashed from the craft accompanied by a piercing ringing sound. A brilliant flash followed and the Porsche exploded.

When questioned later Brooks said he vaguely remembered moving towards Parker when he heard the woman scream. Next thing there was a bright flash and a deafening ringing sound. He clutched his ears, a sensation like vertigo over-came him, sending his head spinning. He fell in a heap.

Police records show Parker and Brooks were found thirty minutes later by PolAir in a highly confused and agitated state. Following questioning by superior officers they were referred to the Disciplinary Tribunal. Once again, they struggled to explain satisfactorily what had transpired. Their vague explanations of what they could remember sounded way too fanciful to their superiors. What added to Brooks' frustration and embarrassment were the constant calls from colleagues of 'Beam me up, Brooksie!'

Both officers were unable to offer a satisfactory explanation for being in possession of such a large quantity of a substance similar to crystal meth and being in a drugged induced state. More concern was raised with the discovery of a hand device on Parker that was found to interfere with traffic lights and radio frequencies. The Crown Prosecutor decided there was insufficient evidence to prosecute both officers, even though they were suspected of covering up a major Ice operation.

No satisfactory explanation was reached regarding the badly damaged Porsche. What was kept confidential under the Federal Government Secrets Act was that the Porsche laboratory tests confirmed the engine was not one of theirs. The vehicle was found to be fuelled by what resembled an ice type substance called bio-variant crystals. Porsche were very disappointed they had to return what was a superior engine and sign a confidentiality agreement.

At a Special Global meeting scientists from various countries raised questions still requiring answers. What else may have been duplicated by these aliens? Who are they? How many are there? How many countries have they infiltrated? How many are among us? Their questions appeared to be endless, and remain unanswered. Due to their persistence in claiming what appears to be an incredible account of what happened to be the truth, no further disciplinary action was taken. But Senior Constable Brooks was demoted to Constable and assigned to clerical duties in Records Management in Police Archives. Constable Parker resigned from the force and is happy driving for an express courier service.

9 780646 948133